# From This Day Forward:

## License Notes

Names, characters, organizations and event portrayed in this novella are either products of the author's imagination or are used fictitiously. Any resemblance to actual events or persons, living or dead, is purely coincidental.

# From This Day Forward:

**Alexandra Medini**

<Alexandra Medini>
<March 2014>

First Printing: <2014>

ISBN <978-1-312-09397-3>

<E. Medinilla >

# Dedication

To my lovely husband.

Thank you. Without your support and patience, I would have never achieved my dream.

<From This Day Forward>

# Chapter 1: The Arrival

Alicia smiled as she looked out the window of the moving car. She couldn't believe how excited she was about this long weekend. Not only had she just gotten a new position as Assistant Manager to one of the most prestigious national wedding apparel companies, "From this Day Forward," but this would be her first time in a classy hotel. She planned to spend her days getting leads, her evenings swimming in the indoor pool, and maybe a massage. As she looked out the window she could see the street was laden with towering hotel buildings. All of them full of happy people arriving and leaving.

"I can't wait to meet the President!" Mindy blurted as she drove the car towards the hotel lobby. "They say that he is very handsome."

Alicia turned towards Mindy; they had become very good friends in the last couple of years. "Yes, well I'm here to work not to go man crazy." She smiled at her best friend.

"Yes, well I'm here to work too, but it won't hurt to look." She had a huge grin from ear to ear as she pulled up behind a large SUV in the valet parking. "Well, here we are, so let get to work."

\*\*\*\*\*\*

"Welcome to sunny Southern California everyone! I hope your stay here will be a magical one," the pilot said over the speakers. "Please make sure your seats are in the upright position and your seat belts are buckled. We have now been cleared for landing."

Jon started to gather all his business contracts and placed them carefully into his suit case. He looked out the plane window and could see all the hotel high rises. Farther out  passed the hotels he could see the bright blue ocean. He would be in Anaheim for a week or so and hoped he could get away from work for a while to sit on the sand. He loved listening to the sound of the waves crashing against the beach. Mostly, he enjoyed watching the color of the sky change at sunset, but he knew that opening a new store would take up most of his time. Between promoting, advertising and training, there would be little time to relax. There never seemed to be time to just simply enjoy life. Jon sighed as he closed his laptop, placed it on top of the contracts in his brief case, and closed the brief case shut.

\*\*\*\*\*\*

After checking in and dropping off their personal belongings in their hotel room, Alicia and Mindy walked over the Anaheim Convention center to set up for the Spring Wedding Show. Although it was May and most of the country was still thawing out from the winter snow, it was a typical day in Anaheim, clear skies, sunny, and warm.  Both women were wearing their best dress suits. Mindy had a plethora to choose from, but Alicia still had not collected that many suits. Her feet hurt as she walked in her new heels. Since her last position had been as a Bridal Specialist who helped the brides try on dresses all day long, she found that wearing flat pumps shoes was easier on her feet. Now that she was in management, however, she needed to look professional.

As they walked into the convection hall Mindy cheered, "I see Mark!" She waved and walked faster towards him. "Doesn't he look good?"

Alicia's stomach churned for a moment she felt nauseous. As Mark dragged the dolly with the mannequins and bridal dresses, she could see his bulging muscles under is truck driver's jump suit. This was not the person she wanted to see today, or ever again for that matter. She slowed her pace down and pretended to be interested in the other booths around the hallway. She hoped that he would be done unloading the items for the show before she arrived at their booth, but no such luck.

"Hello ladies," Mark elongated each vowel with a grin. He looked at Alicia with longing eyes, as he took the dresses off the dolly.

Alicia simply gave him a polite smile, and quickly began to dress the mannequins. *If it looks like I'm busy working, he'll go away and I won't have to talk to him.*

Mandy watched his muscles flexed when he placed the dresses down on the booth table. "Is that everything?" Mindy asked in her usual cheerful voice. She began to check off items on her clip board. "Catalogues, post cards, sample fabric."

Mark couldn't stop staring at Alicia. Suddenly, he realized Mindy was talking to him. He turned towards Mindy, "That's everything that was in the truck. I'll be back on Sunday evening to help you ladies clean up." He looked back at Alicia one last time, hoping to see her beautiful smile, but Alicia kept fussing with the wedding dress on one of the mannequins.

Mindy smiled from ear to ear, "Well, I guess we will see you on Sunday then!" She continued to check off items on her list. When Mark had gone, Mindy turned to Alicia. "Why are you so mean to Mark, you know he has feelings for you?"

Alicia started to hang the fabric samples on the rack next to the booth banner. "Mark reminds me of someone I would rather forget. After that first date, I realized it wouldn't work between us."

Alicia recalled that first and only time they went out. It was just before Valentine's Day. Mark had asked her out, and she had agreed to have dinner with him. She was lonely and tired of staying in every weekend watching television. Plus, she couldn't deny he was well built. You could tell he liked working out. He had broad shoulder and beautiful biceps. He told her he would be by her place at 6 to pick her up for dinner. The only positive of the entire evening was that he has been very prompt. At six o'clock he rang the doorbell. He drove them to a sit down dinner restaurant. When the receptionist asked if they would prefer a table outside or a table by the bar, Mark had immediately responded that he would prefer a table by the bar. While she did not mind sitting by the bar, she felt it would have been nice to be asked what she might like.

Then, when the waitress arrived with the menu, Mark asked her to take the menu away. He already knew what they would be eating. He ordered to plates of medium to well done stakes, with a side of rice and baked potatoes. To drink he told the waitress that they would have two beers. Alicia had to ask the waitress to bring her a glass of ice tea, since she doesn't drink.

While, they waited for their drinks to arrive, Mark was more interest in the football game playing on the big screen above the bar than having a conversation. This was definitely a night she did not want to repeat!

******

I'd better stop by the booth, and see how the set up is going. Jon thought to himself as he pulled up to the hotel. I'll come back to my room and rest once I see that everything is ready for tomorrow morning. He had the bellboy drop off his bags in his room, while he checked in and walked on over to the Convention hall. As he walked closer to his booth, he saw a tall thin blond with a clip board counting catalogues and spreading them all over the table. On the other side he saw a petite long dark haired burnet. She was not as slim as the blond, but she had a nice curvy bottom. "Hello, I'm Jon Whit."

Both Mindy and Alicia turned and looked that the handsome man that stood before them. They both stood motionless, taking in the view. Jon was a tall slender man. He wore a dark gray suit with a silk green tie. You could tell that his outfit was expensive. His eyes were hazel but the green from his tie made them seem greener. His dusty brown hair was short and well trimmed.

Mindy eyes looked like they were about to pop out of her head. "Hello, Mr. Whit. I'm Mindy Sprite. I'm your Newport Beach Store Manager." She turned to Alicia, "This is Alicia Garcia. She is the Assistant Manager."

Alicia smiled and held out her hand. "Hello." She tried to keep her cool, but the butterflies in her stomach wanted out. She hoped that her voice had not revealed her true thoughts, this man is smoking hot!

Jon took her hand. He shook it in a firm but caring way. He knew that greeting a woman was different than greeting a man. There was no need to exert his dominance with a lady. He held her hand as he smiled, his pearly white glistened. "I see you ladies have done an excellent job at setting up the booth. Did everything arrive?"

Mindy looked down to her clip board. "I think so, let me check once more." As she turned the page she noticed the words business cards, but it did not have a check mark. "Oh, no!" Mindy stiffened and her cheeks lost their rosy color.

Alicia quickly pulled her hand away from Jon. She turned and fixated on Mindy. She clenched her fits. "What's wrong?" she asked with a soft voice. Her heart was pounding. She didn't want to make a bad impression. *What if Mr. Whit thinks we are incompetent? Would he replace us?* She didn't want to lose this job. She had just been promoted to Assistant. What if it was something she had done?

"I can't seem to find the business cards." Mindy examined the tables to see if maybe the cards were under the catalogs or post cards.

Alicia quickly started lifting catalogs, but the cards were nowhere in sight. *Why couldn't we have noticed this screw up before he arrived? How do we fix this before he throws us out of the show?"*

Jon noticed that Alicia's light tan face had turned a pale white and Mindy, who was already fair skinned, was as white as paper. He was not surprised by the missing business cards. No show ever went exactly as planned. He had been to enough shows to know that they could wing it without cards. "It's okay, ladies. We can still have a show without cards." He gave them a big grin hoping that would ease the tension.

"I think I have some cards in my purse. If it's not enough I'll just drive over to the shop and pick up some more." Mindy's color returned to her face. Her shoulders relaxed and her usual bubbly demeanor returned. She looked at Mr. Whit. "I'll just go up to the hotel and get my purse."

"Mindy, there is no need to fuss over the cards. We will be fine," Jon insisted.

Mindy's face started to lose its color once more. She stopped breathing, and her body tensed up. She couldn't let it go. This show needed to be perfect, and she knew how to fix the problem, but she couldn't disrespect the President.

Jon noticed the change is Mindy. He quickly reacted, "If you think you have some cards in your purse, why don't you go check."

As soon as he spoke those words of approval, Mindy took off. "I'll see you later!"

Alicia's tan color had returned. She tried not to laugh out loud as she saw her friend all most trip over an older lady down the row. She smirked instead, remembering that Mr. Whit was still standing close by.

"Alicia, have you had dinner yet?" Jon asked. He was tired and hungry, but these ladies had been working hard and had almost had a heart attack over business cards. He thought that food might help lighten the mood.

Alicia didn't know how to respond. She was hungry. Her stomach had started sending the signal, "feed me." They had not eaten since noon, and it was now six. But, she didn't want to have dinner with the President. One screw up a day is all she could handle. *What if I say something stupid? What if he thinks I don't have enough experience to be the Assistant Manger?* She opened her mouth to decline the invitation to dinner. "No, I haven't had dinner."

# Chapter 2: Dinner Proposal

*What have I done!* She couldn't believe she had just agreed to eat dinner with Mr. Whit. Although, she knew that it was by no means a good idea, her body kept telling her differently. She had not been on many dates in her 25 years of life. Between working and keeping a roof over her head, there wasn't much time for men. But she was in a good mood over her new job, and she wanted to go out and have some grown up fun, even if she wouldn't end up in his bed.

"Well then, what would you like to eat, French, Italian, Mexican?" Jon asked with a warm smile. He was having a hard time keeping his eyes off this exquisite little thing.

"I love Mexican food." Alicia responded with a smile and a sparkle in her eyes. She hoped she wasn't being too pushy.

They walked back to the hotel. Alicia tried to break the awkward silence between them. "So Mr. Whit, how long will you be staying here in Southern California?"

"As long as it takes to get your store running smoothly." Jon replied. "And, please call me Jon." He knew it would only take a few days, but this cute little thing was stirring up feelings in him he had not felt in a long time.

When they arrived at the lobby, Jon turned and looked into Alicia's dark honey eyes. She had beautiful long lashes that waved at him as he looked at her. "I'm going to up to my room to change out of this stuffy suit before we go to dinner. Where would you like to meet?"

"I'll wait here in the lobby," Alicia replied. She wanted to check out the spa, and the pool before going to dinner.

When Jon returned to the lobby, he found Alicia sitting in a large hotel lobby chair reading a brochure. She looked so delicate and fragile. For some unknown reason, he wanted to protect her and keep her safe like a piece of fine china. He did not understand these feelings he was having. She was by no means his usual type. In the past, all the women who had caught his eye where tall blond light skinned models. With his job, he didn't have time to go out and meet women so he usually found himself asking a model out from one of the bridal dress photo shoot. He had found that most of the models he had gone out with were self absorbs and greedy.

*I can't believe these spa prices! Well, I guess the spa is out of the question this weekend. I'll just have to spend my evenings by the pool.* Alicia closed up the brochure before looking up. She had been so self-involved that she had not noticed Mr. Whit walking up to her. Suddenly she realized he was staring at her as he walked towards her, she stopped breathing. Her heart began to race and her body began to tingle. *Oh my Goodness!* He had looked hot in a suit, but now he was the perfect man specimen! She could not believe that such a handsome man was taking her to dinner. His baby blue polo shirt left nothing to the imagination. It showed off his toned muscular arms, his broad shoulders and his ribbed torso. The fade blue jeans he wore where tight in all the right places.

"Shall we go?" Jon asked as he put out his hand palm up to help Alicia out of that oversized chair. "I found a Mexican Restaurant online that has received many good reviews. It's called, 'La Cosina,' I thought we might give it a try, unless you know of a better place."

Alicia took his hand and stood up. The scent of his colon was mesmerizing. She had no idea what the food might taste like, at La Cosina, but she didn't care.

She would go anywhere this stud asked her to go. "I guess it well be okay."

Jon let go of her hand as soon as Alicia was stable. He didn't want to come on too hard. He looked around the lobby and asked, "Will Mindy be joining us for dinner?" hoping the answer would be no.

"She texted me that she was headed back to the shop to pick up some business cards, to go on without her." Alicia tried not to show how pleased she was with the fact that she would have this delicious eye candy all to herself this evening.

"The car is outside." Jon motioned towards the door.

# Chapter 3: Desert Anyone?

As Jon drove to the restaurant, he wanted to know all about Alicia. This was the perfect time to learn more. "So how do you like being the Assistant Manager?" He thought he should start with easy questions.

Alicia bit her lower lip. *How do I answer that question without letting on that I'm scared to death?* "Well so far, it's been a nice experience." I hope he didn't hear the hesitation.

"How long have you been working with us?" Jon hoped the question didn't sound like interrogation. He continued looking at the traffic, although he now wished he had called for a taxi instead so he could gaze into her beautiful eyes.

"I have been working for the company for about three years, as a Bridal Specialist." She hoped that would end the interrogation. She decided it was time to have him answer instead. "Do you travel a lot?"

"I guess you would say that I do. I travel to many of the Bridal Shows and visit shops as often as I can." Jon didn't want to talk about himself. He wanted to know more about her.

****** 

The restaurant was right on the beach. As they walked up the board walk towards the front door, they could hear the live Cumbia music. Jon noticed that Alicia suddenly developed an extra bounce in her step, and the smile on her face was shining brighter. It pleased him to see that Alicia was having fun, something he never had time for. Jon held the door open for her as they walked inside.

In the center of the restaurant was a small stage and dance floor. The tables lined up against the outer walls, and on the beach side, the entire wall had been replaced by floor to wall windows.

Jon leaned down and whispered close to her ear, "Would you mind if we sat by the window?"

Alicia's body burst into flames. She leaned in towards him. She felt his breathing close to her ear and it set her body on fire. She felt goose bumps run up her spine. *I'll sit on your lap if you ask me too.* She nodded, and whispered "Yes."

Jon asked for a table by the window. The view of the sun setting on the ocean was spectacular. The waves crashed into the sand and the sky was a myriad of red and orange hues. He pulled out the chair for her, and helped her sit down. The way the sun kissed Alicia's tanned skin made her glow. He watched as she swayed to the music and perused the menu. Jon could not remember a more perfect view. A wave of happiness came over him.

"Hi, I'm Nancy. What would you like to drink this evening?"

"I will have a bottle of your best wine, and two glasses. Is that okay with you, Alicia?" He asked.

"I would prefer an ice tea, Mr. Whit." She didn't want to sound ungrateful, but she did not like drinking.

"That is fine. Nancy, please bring the wine and an ice tea. Thank you. Now Alicia, there is something we need to definitely discuss." He spoke in his firm business voice, and gave her a no joking stare.

Alicia was surprised by this sudden change in tone. She stopped swaying and stopped breathing. She felt her body tensed up as she put down the menu. She met Mr. Whit's stern eyes. *Oh no, what did I say?* "What do we need to discuss?"

"You keep calling me Mr. Whit," I would prefer that you call me Jon. "Do you think you can do that?"

Alicia sighed. She took a deep breath, "Mr. Whit, you are my boss. I am your employee. I don't feel comfortable calling you by your first name. We are not equals. Sometimes it is hard for people to understand, but I was raised in a strict Catholic home where everyone knew their place, and we were not allowed to be disrespectful." She lowered her eyes and glanced at her menu and then back at Mr. Whit.

"I see. So you will not call me Jon because I am your boss. Well, I can respect that, but you are forgetting..."

Alicia was sure he was about to fire her. She tightened her jaw and braced for it.

"I am technically not your boss. Most store are independent franchises. I cannot fire you, only the shop owner can do that. Second, it's after hours and we are not at work. Right now I am just a man having dinner with a beautiful woman. So, please call me Jon. Tomorrow between eight o'clock and six o'clock you can call me Mr. Whit, if you like. Does that sound fair?" Jon couldn't believe was trying to negotiate a deal for name calling.

Alicia was stunned. *Did he just say I was beautiful?* She felt the heat in her cheeks rise. She tilted her head towards her left shoulder, looked into those beautiful hazel eyes and nodded in agreement.

"Here are your drinks. Are you ready to order?"

"Have decided what you would like to eat?" Jon asked as he realized he had not yet looked at the menu. He quickly opened it to see what he was in the mood for. Although the only thing he really wanted to taste was Alicia's sweet savory lips.

"Yes, I think I will have a plate of Sopes, please." *With a side order of Mr. Hunk!* She closed the menu and handed it back to Nancy.

"I guess, I'll have the same," Jon added as he closed the menu. "So Alicia, tell me about yourself, are you married?" He looked at her with eager anticipation.

Alicia laughed and shook her head, "No, I'm not married," She looked down at her tea and swirled the ice around with the straw. Then she tilted her head and lifted her eyes to meet his. In a soft voice she added, "And I'm not seeing anyone at the moment." *I hope that wasn't too forward.*

That declaration of singleness, send Jon's heart into over drive. *Did she just say she's available?* Jon tried not to smile at the thought that he might be able to kiss her. He quickly turned away hoping that she had not been able to read his thoughts. He glanced out the windows to watch as the sun set over the ocean. "What about your family? Do they live nearby?"

Alicia's lower lip pouted. "I don't have any family, not anymore." She sank back into her chair. She turned to watch the sun set and started to recall her past.

Jon brought his attention back towards Alicia. He tilted his head and gave her a questioned look.

*Snap out of it! Don't be stupid! This is a beautiful evening. You just got promoted. The view is to die for and the music is awesome.* She quickly put on a smile, sat up straight and said, "Let's just say I have lost touch with them. What about you, are you married?"

Jon grinned. "No, and I'm not seeing anyone at the moment."

The sound of the music seemed to have gotten louder, couples started gathering on the dance floor. Alicia was having a hard time staying in her seat. She loved dancing, especially to Cumbia music. Her heart began to beat to the sound of the drums, and her soul began to scream for her to move. "Mr. Whit, I mean Jon, do you dance?"

Jon laughed a nervous laugh. "I don't dance. In my thirty years of life I have never gotten around to learning." He hoped that she would not ask him to dance. He knew that he would not be able to say no to her, but he didn't want to look like a fool.

Alicia looked intensely into his eyes trying to figure a way to get him onto the dance floor without having to beg. She placed both hands on the table and leaned forwards towards him. "Well, Jon I have never gotten around to drinking wine. So, if you teach me how to appreciate wine, then I'll teach you how to have some fun on the dance floor." She smiled with a smirk on her face.

Jon laughed. This gal knows how to bargain! "Sounds fair." He stood up and asked, "May I have this dance?"

Alicia jumped at the chance to dance. She held his hand as he led her to the dance floor. As soon as her feet touched the dance floor, her hips let loose. She swung her hips from side to side. Her shoulders rotated back and forth, and the way she swayed her head made her long dark hair bounced. She smiled and teased Jon with her eyes. Jon tried to move to the beat of the music. Then, suddenly he froze, fascinate by the way she moved. *She's so hot.* He especially loved the way she shook her ass!

Alicia realized that Jon was mesmerized by her. She could see the lust in his eyes. She started to blush, but she wasn't about to sit down. She loved dancing too much. She swung around so she could not see him staring at her. She also wanted to give him a better view of her 'ass'ets. Sometimes having a pear shape body had its pluses.

Soon, dinner arrived and they sat back down to eat. Jon asked for a second wine glass. He poured the wine. He swirled it, sniffed then tasted it. A smile came over his lips. He moaned and said, "Very sweet."

Alicia gave him a crooked smile. She couldn't tell if he was talking about the wine, or her. Once more she began to feel her cheeks redden. "Okay, I guess it's my turn to give it a try." She swirled the wine, sniffed it and tasted it. She had no idea why you were expected to swirl and sniff before you drank it, but when in Rome, do as the Romans. She swallowed. The darn thing burned the inside of her throat. She felt it burning all the way down to her stomach. Needless to say, she didn't like it. She made a sour face.

Jon couldn't help but laugh.

# Chapter 4: A Good Night Kiss

Around ten in the evening, they decided it was time to head back. The Show would start early and they would be on their feet all day. As they walked out onto the boardwalk, Alicia felt the cold ocean breeze on her shoulders and bear arms. She had left her blazer in the car and was suddenly cold. She rubbed her hand over her arm to warm it. Not paying attention to the boardwalk slabs, her heel got stuck between two slabs, and she started to fall forward.

Jon immediately reacted. He jumped in front of her and caught her in his arms. "Are you okay?" He asked with sincere concern.

She grabbed his fore arms to steady herself. *Darn, those are some toned muscles.* "My shoe got stuck." With her foot she jiggled the shoe free.

As she straightened herself, Jon came in closer. He placed his left hand on her lower back to help her stabilize. He could no longer control himself. He took his right hand and placed it under her chin. He pulled her face in closer to his. Then, he leaned down and stole a soft kiss off her sweet luscious lips. As soon as he had, he realized he was way out of line. He pulled his head back and looked at Alicia, expecting to be slapped.

"I..." Jon didn't know how he wanted to finish this sentence. Should he apologize for being so forward or should he tell her how attractive she was.

Alicia was momentarily paralyzed. She felt Jon's warm body shielding her from the cool breeze. It felt wonderful. When his soft lips touched hers, they had aroused something deep down south of the boarder inside her. She didn't know how to react; all she knew was that at that moment she didn't want him to let her go.

"Thank you... for catching me. I didn't want to end up kissing the floor." *Oh my Goodness, I can't believe I just said that. So lame!* She couldn't get her body to move away from his.

Jon dropped his right hand and took a step back to give her some space. As he moved he felt her shiver. "Are you okay? You seem to be shaking?"

Alicia realized that she was still cold and she pulled away from Jon. She rubbed her arms with her hands. "I forgot my blazer in the car, and I'm little cold. I'll be fine as soon as we get in the car." She turned away from Jon and began to walk back to the car.

Jon was not about to let this opportunity to touch her get away. He wrapped his right arm around her shoulder and pressed closer into her body. "I don't have a coat to offer you, but I can offer you some warmth."

Alicia smiled as they walked back the car. His scent was intoxicating. The warmth that radiated off his strapping torso and the strength in his arms, were driving Alicia crazy. She had slept with very few men in her life time, but this man, she wanted him badly. *Oh, he's such a 'mango.' I just want to eat him up. I must be insane! I can't just throw myself at him. He's still the President.*

As Jon opened the car door for Alicia, she leaned in and kissed him on the cheek. "Thank you for a lovely dinner."

Jon stood and put his hand on her lower back. He gazed into her honey eyes. In a low soft voice he said, "Thank you, Alicia for a memorable evening. I don't get to enjoy as much time as I would like watching the sunset and having some fun. This evening will be something I will cherish for a long time." He was unsure if she would allow him the kiss her, but he couldn't contain his hunger for her any longer. He looked at those soft lips that seemed to call to him. He leaned in for a kiss and was gladly surprised she kissed him back. He wrapped his arms around her.

Alicia's world started to rock. Her body was on fire. She wanted him. *Oh my Goodness, Oh my Goodness, Oh my Goodness*! He tastes so good. She wanted to pull in closer to feel all of him. She placed her hands on his hard pecks, and then pulled back. "Jon."

Jon pulled his lips away from her and looked at her.

"I think, we should go now, we have to be at the show early tomorrow." She pulled away from his strong arms, and climbed into the car.

Jon closed the car door, and took a moment to compose himself. *I can't figure her out. Is she toying with me? Or am I miss reading her?* He walked around the car and started back to the hotel.

******

Alicia had picked up the Spa Brochure off the car seat before she sat down. She gripped it with a tight fit. That brochure was the only thing stopping her from running her fingers thought Jon's hair. She didn't know what to say to break the awful silence. She kept her eyes on the road afraid that if she looked at him, she would not be able to stop herself from going all the way with him.

Jon glanced over towards her and noticed the Spa Brochure she was holding in her left hand. "What is that?" he asked nonchalantly.

Alicia looked down at the Brochure, "Oh, this is a Spa Brochure I picked up in the lobby. I thought I might get a massage before the weekend is over, but I didn't realize that it was an exclusive club."

Jon kept his eyes on the road. "I didn't they had an exclusive club."

A smile came over Alicia's face as she laughed. "It's not a truly exclusive club. I just meant that you need to have money to pay for these ridiculous prices, so in a sense most regular people can't get in." She stopped for a moment to think. "Guess I'll just have to add it to my goal poster for this year."

"What is a goal poster?"

"Oh, I made goal posters for all the bride specialists. I asked everyone to write down what they want to accomplish by the end of the year. Every day before we open the store, we all take a moment to read our goals. If we want to add to the poster we can. If someone has met their goal we celebrate with hugs." Alicia seemed to relax as she thought about work.

"Sounds like you are an awesome manager." Jon complimented her with pride in his tone. "I'm glad that you are a part of the 'From this Day Forward' family."

When they arrived at the hotel, the valet took the car. They shared an elevator up. Alicia's room was on the 15th floor. When the door opened, she turned to Jon and smiled. "Good night." Then stepped out and walked to her room.

Leaving him had been difficult. She wanted so badly to grab him in the elevator and have her way with him. It had taken all her strength to avoid looking at him. She could not afford to get fired. Living on the streets had not been easy and she never planned to end up there again. So, if it meant avoiding Jon for the rest of the weekend, then that is what she would do.

When she entered her room Mindy was already in her bed. The room was dark and Alicia tried not to make any noise.

"Do you know what time it is young lady?" Mindy teased has she turned on the lamp light. "Where have you been?"

"I went to dinner, remember." Alicia tried to sound casual as she sat down on her bed and removed those painful heels. She rubbed her throbbing feet. She hated high heels.

Mindy squinted her eyes and her, "You expect me to believe that you where at dinner this whole time?"

"Well, we also danced." Alicia grinned.

"Oh, now you have to tell me everything!" Mindy sat up on her bed ready for a bed time story.

Alicia got ready for bed and told Mindy most of what happened that evening. She decided that telling her about the kissing was not really necessary so she skipped over that part. Besides those kisses were hers and she would treasure them like golden nuggets.

# Chapter 5: The Bridal Show

The first day of the show was electrifying. At nine in the morning, the Convention hall filled with happy and excited brides to be. Mindy and Alicia spent most of the day handing out catalogues, business cards, and setting up appointments. Jon stood around and simply watched as the dynamic duo wooed the crowd. He was impressed in their ability to relate to all the potential customers. By lunch time the two of them had already set up 20 appointments. Jon was delighted and quite pleased. He loved having successful shops, and this event would put the Newport Beach shop in the black.

Jon went back into the convention center to find lunch while Mindy and Alicia continued to mingle and work the crowd. He brought back some deli turkey sandwiches and two side orders of baked sweet potato fries, along with two tall cups of ice tea.

"Alicia, I bought lunch," Jon handed her the white bag and a tray with two tall cups. "Please take a break and eat. I'll stay here and pass out catalogues."

Alicia smiled, "Thank you Mr. Whit. I guess I can take a moment to eat. As she reached to take the bag, her hand brushed over his. She started to blush.

Mindy notice how Mr. Whit had been admiring Alicia all morning. As she walked up to them, she could see how Alicia was blushing. Mindy grinned. "So, what's going on?" she asked in a teasing voice.

Alicia turned to her with a stare that said I want to kill you. "We're taking a lunch break." She turned and walked way.

Mindy smiled at Mr. Whit. "I guess you're on your own for a while. Alicia, wait up!"

Jon smiled back at Mindy and watched Alicia's ass as she walked away. Nice view.

"So, what's going on between you two?" Mindy asked as they sat down to eat outside the Show Hall.

"There is nothing going on." Alicia pulled out her sandwich and took a bite. She tried to keep a straight face.

"So, the fact that Mr. Whit has been following you around with puppy eyes all day doesn't mean anything?" Mindy put a fry in her mouth.

"I have no idea why you think he's been following me around." Alicia kept eating.

"Okay, if you don't want to talk about it." Mindy knew Alicia would sooner or later spill her guts out so she'd let it go for now. "I thought this evening we could go over to the bar and see what happens." She took another fry.

"I plan to take a swim this evening. You, know I don't drink." Alicia relied.

"Yes, I know that. I also know that's why you haven't been laid in over two years." Mindy said bawdily.

Alicia gave Mindy that, I want to kill you, look again. "In any case, I would rather spend my evening swimming and reading than having to deal with a bunch of mindless drunks who simply want to get into my pants."

They both laughed. "We should head on back."

The rest of the day was just as busy as the morning, more brides, more appointments, more handing out catalogues. When the show closed for the evening, they were all ready to get out and relax.

As they all walked back to the hotel, Jon smiled at both Mindy and Alicia, "Ladies, you did an excellent job today." He looked tired, but still in a good mood. "Would you ladies like to go get some dinner?"

Mindy quickly responded with a grin from ear to ear, "I'm planning on going to the bar for dinner.

Would you like to join me? Alicia's not interested in bars so she has decided not to go. She thinks hanging out at the pool would be better."

Jon thought about it for a moment. "Thank you for the invitation Mindy, but I think I should probably stay in and return some phone calls. Good night then." He headed for the elevator.

Alicia and Mindy took a different elevator up to their room.

# Chapter 6: Fireworks

Jon had changed out of his stuffy suit and into his training clothes. He planned to hit the gym before going to bed this evening. He sat at the desk by the suite window. He was going through his emails when an image of Alicia's smile popped into his head. He remembered how she had blushed when their hands had accidently touched at lunch time. He shook his head hoping to shake her image out of his mind. *Too much work to think about a girl.* He went back to his emails.

When all emails had been addressed Jon headed for the hotel gym.

******

Alicia had gotten a green chicken salad on the way to the pool. She had already taken 8 laps in the deep side before eating her salad. Now she relaxed with a book. She had decided that this week she would read The 7 Habits of Highly Effective People.

As Jon approached the gym entrance, he noticed that Alicia was sitting in a lounge chair. She looked like a tempting chocolate kiss, small but quite tantalizing. Her dark damp hair framed her face and landed on her well placed breasts. Her one piece swimsuit showed off all her curves. Jon was drawn to her like a magnet. He couldn't stop himself. He didn't know why, but he wanted her.

Jon sat down in the lounge chair next to Alicia. "Hi! Is that book any good?" He had already read it but he wanted to know her take on it.

Alicia looked over at him from behind her book. *Oh god, I look a mess!* "Well, I just started reading so I don't really know. What are you doing here?" She tried to redirect the questions hoping she could drive him away before he noticed how badly she looked in a bathing suit.

"I was headed for the gym when I saw you and thought I'd ask what you thought of this book." Jon tried to keep his eyes on hers and not make it so obvious that he was checking her out.

"I really don't have an opinion just yet, I really just started reading it. If they had the movie version, I might watch it instead." Alicia replied honestly.

Jon bent his head back and laughed. "I haven't been to the movies in ten years, but I know that this book would not be a block buster!"

Alicia couldn't believe that Jon had not been to the movies in such a long time. She was about to comment, when a child two lounge chairs way dropped a glass cup. The loud smashing sound caught Alicia off guard and instantly she jumped. "Oh my!"

Jon noticed how she had reacted to the loudness. "It's okay. It's just glass." He reached and touched her arm.

Immediately Alicia nerves clamed. "Sorry, I did mean to react that way. I just seem to have a problem with loud noises. You should have seen me last night. I thought we were under attack by foreign enemies. I didn't know that there would be fireworks over head."

Jon kept his hand on her. "You mean the fireworks from the happiest place on earth?"

"Yes, Mindy had to convince me that we were not being invaded. I went to the window to see the fireworks, but our room faces the opposite direction. So, I was unable to see the show." She signed. "Maybe I should add that to my goal's poster as well."

All of the sudden Jon had a marvelous idea, one that would get Alicia to spend time with him and him alone. "Since I have not been to the movies in an obviously a long time, and you have never seen the Magical Fireworks, what if you join me for movie night. My suite faces the Magic Kingdom, and has a nonintrusive view of the fireworks. You get to pick the movie." He gave her a one sided smile.

Alicia didn't know what to say. Is *he asking up to his suite? Oh my!* "Well, if you plan to have a movie night, everyone knows you need to have popcorn." Her eyes sparkled and teased Jon.

"Okay, I'll stop by the gift shop and pick up a bag of popcorn." He stood and held out his hand to help Alicia out of her seat.

*What have I done? I don't know how long I can stop myself from taking his close off.* Alicia stood up and wrapped a towel around. All that showed where her arms and the legs. Everything that Jon wanted to look at was covered. "Okay, but it may take me an hour to change and dry my hair."

Jon's heart started to pound. "I'll see you in an hour." He turned and walked away.

Alicia stared as Jon's firm butt as he walked away. *Oh, I just want to squeeze those buns!*

\*\*\*\*\*\*

As Alicia arrived to the door of the suite, she stopped and ran her hands through her hair. Not because it needed brushing, she had just spent 20 minutes drying it, but to release her nervousness. The other 20 minutes she had spent deciding what she would wear. She couldn't decide between jeans or a dress. She had finally decided to go with her black and white striped pattern maxi dress. It had a scooped neckline, a racer-back and sleeveless. Not much of an evening out dress, but was better than her torn jeans. Plus, it accentuated all her curves. She knocked.

It seemed as if Jon had been standing behind the door. She had not finished knocking when the door opened. "Glad you made it!" Jon said as he stepped back and he motioned for her to come in.

Alicia couldn't believe how large the suite was. The living room area was three times larger than their room alone. The wall opposite the hallway was all glass, and you could see the Magic Kingdom from it. To her right was the kitchenette and next to the kitchenettes was a door that was closed. To the left was a huge flat screen television. It was half the size of the wall. By the window wall, was a desk where Jon had obviously set up his personal office. "Wow, what a view!" Alicia's eyes were drawn to the window. She walked towards it. "Have you ever been to the Small world?"

Jon just stood and watched her walk towards the window. *I wonder how long it would take for me to take that dress off?* "When I was little my mom would take my brother and me to the magic kingdom while my dad went to the show. He walked into the kitchenette.

"You, have a brother." Alicia eye brows rose with curiosity.

"Yep, he's my baby brother and the vice president. He also lives in Michigan with his wife Sara and two kids." Deep down Jon was jealous of his brother's family life. He wished he could have time to fall in love, marry and start a family. Quickly he changed the subject before Alicia could realize the resentment he felt towards his only kin.

"I couldn't find popcorn in the gift shop so I had to order out." He said as he tried to remember he had to be a gentleman. He went into the kitchenette and brought out a large serving tray.

The tray had six large bags of popcorn. "I didn't know which you would like, so I ordered one of each." Jon hoped that Alicia would find a flavor she liked. He set the tray down on the coffee table between the sofa and the television.

Alicia turn back to face him as he was placing the tray down on the table. He had changed out of his sexy workout outfit and was now wearing his jeans and a white polo shirt. Alicia could just stand there all night and enjoy the view, but when Jon stood up, she had to stop staring.

She walked over to the table and looked at all the gourmet popcorn on the table. There was a large bag of Cheddar Popcorn, Premium Caramel Popcorn, Chocolate Salted Caramel, Butter Toffee with Almonds, Jalapeño, and Tuxedo Popcorn. She smiled, "Most of the time, I just eat the microwavable kind."

Jon, didn't know what to say. He stood there unable to figure out what to do. He hoped that Alicia didn't think he was a snob.

Alicia noticed that Jon's demeanor had changed. He seemed a little standoffish. Quickly she tried to save the mood. "I think I'll try them all." She sat down in front of the coffee table and grabbed the Tuxedo bag.

Jon sat next to her, "Which did you want to start with." He leaned in towards her see which she had chosen. "Mmm, Tuxedo. Can I have some?"

Alicia passes the bag to him. She reached down and took the TV remote. "I thought we might watch The Interns. Have you seen that one?"

"No, I haven't seen anything in the last ten years." The only thing Jon wanted to watch was Alicia, but if he had to sit through a boring movie to keep her there with him, he was willing to sit through it.

"I like this movie, because it reminds me a little of me." Alicia said as she leaned back and got comfortable in the large soft sofa.

Jon, sat back, turned the lights down and watched the movie. They shared popcorn and they laughed though out the movie. He leaned in so his shoulders were touching hers. He could smell Alicia's coconut shampoo and it was turning him on.

Alicia tried to act casual, but having Jon so close was sending shock waves through her entire body. Eating popcorn and watching a movie was the last thing she wanted to do. *He's still the President and way out of my league. Don't be stupid, he could still figure out a way to fire you.*

The movie was just about over when the first boom sounded. Alicia jumped and popcorn flew out of the third bag. "Sorry." She turned to the window. The fireworks had started. She quickly got up and walked up to the large windows. She could see the bright colors of the fireworks. Each boom brought about a plethora of color. "It's beautiful!" she whispered.

Jon could no longer control his desire. He walked up behind Alicia and wrapped his arms around her waist. He leaned down where his lips could touch her left ear. He took a deep breath of her scent, "Nothing is as beautiful as you," he whispered.

Alicia closed her eyes and leaned back into him. She could no long stand the yearning she felt within her. She wanted to feel every part of his muscular body. She wanted to taste him, and run her tongue all over. She began to breathe heavily.

Jon knew he could now make his move. She hadn't rejected him. He placed his hands on her hips and turned her around. Now they were face to face. Softly Jon kissed her bottom lip. Alicia wrapped her arms around Jon's neck. She ran her fingers through his short hair. Jon tightened his grip around her waist. Soon Jon had found his way into her mouth. He wanted to explore her, all of her even her mouth.

"Jon, I..." Alicia pulled her head way from Jon.

Jon looked at her with his hazel wanting eyes. He didn't release her from his arms. He looked at her, waiting to hear what it was she wanted. At that moment he would do anything she asked of him. Even though, he wanted her, he would leave if she asked.

Alicia didn't know how to finish her sentence. She could feel her heart bounding just as loudly as his. She body wanted him. *Screw reason! I can kick myself in the morning!* With her right hand she pulled his head towards her. She looked at his soft lips and moved in to kiss him.

Jon understood. He moved his hand up her back and press her chest into his body. Alicia's breathing became ragged. She took her leg and slid it up Jon's thigh. Jon took that as a sign. He grabbed her thigh and ran his hand up to her ass. He took his lips and started kissing her neck. He wanted to taste her, to feel her. "Alicia, I want to taste you." He moaned. He looked at her to see her reaction.

Alicia didn't know what to say. She wanted him just as bad. She reached to remove his shirt and he raised his hands to help. She ran her fingers over his chest hair. "Then, you should probably show me to the bedroom."

Jon took in a deep breath. He took her by the hand an escorted her into the closed door. The room was dark but the bright lights of the city and and the full moon filled the room with a dim light. The silhouette of a king size bed took up most of the room.

Alicia smiled. "That's some bed."

Before she could continue her sentence, Jon wrapped his hand around her and started kissing the back of her neck. "You smell, delicious." His breathing had become ragged. He turned her around and looked down at her breast. He wanted to play with her. He carefully placed her on the edge of the bed and ran his hand down the side her hips. When he reached the bottom of her dress he ran his hand up to feel her skin. Alicia's body was ignited; her whole body was engulfed in flames. She helped Jon take her dress off. She wasn't wearing a bra since her dress had one sewn into it. She lay there with only her panties between them, her nipples at attention.

At that moment, she became self conscious. She knew she was nowhere close to having the prefect body. She felt vulnerable, and uneasy.

Jon stood up and removed his pants along with his boxers. He was fully aroused. Alicia could not believe how handsome and taut he was. She couldn't believe how arouse he was. *He seriously wants me.* He climbed on top of her and he ran his hand though her hair. He kissed her nipple before he took it into his mouth. Alicia wrapper her legs around Jon's torso and she put her hands in his hair. His tongue was causing her whole body to throb. She arched her back and moaned.

Jon smiled at the sound of her moaning. He wanted her to feel how much he wanted her. He released one nipple and took the other one. Alicia continued to shake beneath him. He took his hand and ran it down her stomach and right between her thighs. Realizing her panties were still in his way, he carefully pulled them off. He stood there at the edge of the bed and moaned. "MMM."

Alicia was also enjoying the view. She could not believe that this demigod wanted her. She felt excited and vulnerable all at once. Jon turned and walked over the night stand. "Jon?"

"I'll be right there." Jon grabbed a condom from his nightstand and put it on. He returned to the edge of the bed. "Now where were we?" He climbed between her legs, slowly penetrating her, and moaning every inch.

Alicia's body shook in pleasure. Alicia reached up with both hands to feel his hot and sweaty chest. She had never felt this inflamed before. Jon was driving her body and soul mad with want. She wanted him fully in her. She wrapped her legs around his ass and pressed him towards her. She began to gyrate her hips.

"Oh, baby it feels warm in here." Jon whispered and he leaned forward near her ear. "Come of me baby," he ordered, and he kissed her neck.

Alicia's body finally exploded into a climax. She yelled a loud intense moan, then collapsed under

Jon's body. For a few seconds Alicia stopped breathing. "Oh, my," where the words out of her mouth once she remembered she needed to breath.

Jon was still inside her and still as hard and a rock. He laid on top of her and rolled over so that he was on the bottom and she was on top. He looked up at her body, and bit down on his lower lip, his eyes devouring her inch by inch. He loved the way her hair caresses her perfectly formed breasts. He loved how his hands felt around her voluminous butt. Just looking at her made him almost pop. He used his hands to lift her and bring her back down on him.

Alicia leaned down and kissed him before placing her hands on his chest and following his cue. Alice slowly and methodically lowered and lifted herself. She could hear Jon's moaning getting louder and more uncontrollable. Finally, he let out a loud grunt, pulled her towards him and kissed her with a passionate kiss. He pulled out, but did not let her go. He took the condom and dropped it into the trash can next to the night stand.

Alicia laid in Jon's arms in complete ecstasy. No man had ever made her feel the way Jon had. His manly scent was captivating, his body was delicious, his thoughtfulness was hypnotic. This would be a night she would never be able to forget. Her naked body began to shiver as she started to cool down.

"Alicia, are you okay?" Jon could feel her shaking.

"I'm starting to feel a little chilly. I think I should probably get dresses and go." She tried to get up, but Jon would not release her.

"Don't go." Jon whispered. He reached over his head and pulled down the covers so Alicia could get warmed.

Alicia tried to convince herself to leave. "Mindy will be worried, if I don't show up."

Jon sat up on the bed. He reached over the nightstand and took his phone. Alicia quickly sat up next to him. "What are you doing?" she asked with a worried tone.

"I'm texting Mindy telling her you are here with me." Jon replied.

Quickly Alicia put her hand over the phone. "No, don't."

Jon looked at her with hurt eyes, "Why?"

"I don't want her to know that I am here with you," her voice softened as she spoke.

Again Jon questioned with a hurt tone, "Why?"

Alicia took a deep breath, "Jon this has been the best night of my life, but you are only here for a few weeks, then you will be gone. You have nothing to lose, but I do. I can't afford to lose my job and my reputation. That is all I have. I know I'm just one of many women who have shared you bed and ..." Alicia decided to stop before she made a total fool of herself.

Jon put the phone back on the nightstand. He ran his hand along Alicia's jaw bone and kissed her softly, then looked directly into her beautiful eyes. "Alicia, I would never do anything to hurt you intentionally. Please know that. You make me feel alive, like there is a purpose to my life, and you are not just another woman that I have shared my bed with. You are the first woman I have allowed into my bed in a very long time. I don't tend to sleep around."

Alicia smiled wanting to believe every single word he said. Her body and soul believed him, but her logical brain knew this could not work. Happiness and sadness filled her. She did not move. She did not know what to say.

Jon jumped up out of bed, "I'll be right back." He walked back into the living room.

Alicia had a perfect view of his perfect ass. *OMG I just want to sink my teeth into those firm buns.*

Jon quickly returned with her purse in his hand. "Here," he handed it to her.

Alicia did not understand. "Do you want me to leave now?" she asked confused.

Jon laughed, "No, hell no. I want you to text Mindy. Tell her you met a stud and are spending the night with him," a playful grin came over Jon's face.

Alicia laughed, "A stud?"

Jon opened her purse and took out her phone, "Well if you won't I will." He started texting.

Alicia could not believe that he wanted her to spend the night. She shook her head in disapproval, but Jon did not care. "There, it's done. Now where were we?" He rolled Alicia under the covers and held her close. He wanted her as close as was humanly possible.

Alicia draped her hand over his torso, and kisses in neck. "Goodnight." She closed her eyes and fell into a deep sleep.

# Chapter 7: The Other Woman

When Alicia woke, she realized she was alone in that huge bed. She felt around with her hands, but he was not there. She sat up and remembered she needed to be at the show. Quickly she ran into the bathroom and took a shower. She dressed and came into the living room. Jon was sitting by the window working on his lap top. He was already fully dress in his business suit.

He stood and walked towards her. "Good morning. I ordered breakfast. I hope you like it." He kissed her slowly and deliberately taking a whiff of her hair. "It's over here is the kitchenette."

*He so sweet.* "Thank you." Alicia said before she knew what he had ordered. She looked on the table and there was a large breakfast burrito.

"It has eggs, tomatoes, beans and rice." Jon stated proudly. "Now, I have to go to the Show, but you are welcome to stay here and enjoy her breakfast."

"What time it is?" Alicia asked in a frantic voice. She was mad at herself for losing track of time.

"Fifteen minutes to nine." Jon said as kissed her head and headed for the door. "No, good for both of us to be late, I'll see you later." Jon waved and closed the door behind him.

Alicia grabbed her burrito, and ran into the bedroom for her purse. She ran out of the suite and into the next elevator. The only good thing about being late to the show was that Mindy would not be in their room when she arrived. She knew that Mindy would interrogate her as soon as she had a chance. When she reached her room she opened her purse to take out her door key card. She couldn't believe what she found. Inside her purse where two key cards, one card had a sticky note attached to it. The note was hand written,

"Please come back." She could not believe that Jon had given her a key to his suite. She tried not to cry. *How can he possibly want me?*

She ran inside and changed into her business suit, then tried to sprint in heels all the way into the Convention Hall. It was nine thirty when she arrived at the booth. Mindy and Jon were both busy mingling with a wave of soon to be brides. Alicia grabbed a stack of catalogues and started passing them out. Mindy looked over towards her and gave her a frowned look. Alicia mouthed a "Sorry" to Mindy behind Jon's back.

When Jon had finished talking to a prospective customer, Alicia approached him, "Mr. Whit, I am truly sorry about being late this morning. I can assure you, it will not happen again."

Jon could see the concern in her eyes. "I'm sure it could not be helped," Jon replied with a smile on his face. Then, he winked at her.

The rest of the morning was just at busy as the day before. At lunch time Mindy and Alicia headed to the deli outside the hall. As they sat down with their chicken salads, Mindy could no longer hold in her curiosity.

"So, I got your message this morning. You stayed out all night, and by the glow in your cheeks, you finally got laid. So tell me about the man who pinned you down." Mindy grinned as she took a sip of her tea.

"I can't tell you, who he is, but I can tell you that it was an amazing night." Alicia started to blush.

"Ooo, a nameless man, that just means you did it with a married man," Mindy's eye brows raised waiting for Alicia to confirm her suspicions.

"I hope he's not married," she sighed as she played with her lettuce.

"Well, are you going to see him again tonight, or was it a one night thing?" Mindy eyes were fixed on Alicia like a dog on a bone. She wasn't going to let up.

"I don't know yet." Alicia reasoned with anguish in her voice.

Mindy reached over the table and put her hand over Alicia's. "Why, is it so hard for you to let someone in? Just follow your heart, silly, or your girl parts, which ever are louder."

Alicia laughed. "You dork!" Mindy always knew what to say to make feel better.

"Well, if you are going out again, I need to know so I have my options open. I mean if you plan to be gone all night that means I can party in our room. So, please let me know." She started eating her salad. That was all that was said about her mysterious man.

Soon after they returned from lunch, a tall supermodel blond started to wave that Ms. America wave, "Oh, Jon. I can't believe it's you!"

Alicia, Mindy and Jon were all stunned. This woman was a size two, with a black mini shirt that showed off her long slender and well shaped legs. In bright red stiletto heels she headed towards them, obviously locked onto her target. Her breast arrived and presses up against Jon's chest ten seconds before she did. She wrapped her arms around his neck and planted a well meant kiss on his lips.

Bewildered, Jon stood still with his hands parallel to his body. He pulled his head back. "Janet?"

"Oh Jon, why didn't you call me when you arrived," she said with a smiled that showed her perfect bright white smile. She arms moved down from Jon's neck and landed her slim hand on his chest.

"Hey, girls come over here," Janet waved over to direct the attention of two other runway models. "I want you to meet my friends," she squealed as she wrapped her arm around Jon's arm.

"Cindy and Katrina, this is Jon Whit, the President of "From this Day Forward," Janet rested her head on Jon's shoulder as the other two women approached and surrounded him.

"What are you doing here Janet?" Jon lifted his shoulder to remove Janet's head from where she rested it. She took the hint but when Jon tried to pull away Janet didn't let go.

"Well, Katrina here is tying the knot and we came here to look at our options. I can't believe it's been a year since we have spoken." She took her loose hand ran it up Jon's lapel and gave him a stare that said I want you.

"Jon, why don't you go to lunch with us and you can tell Katrina about all the wonderful dress options she has available at you shops," her eyes sparkled.

"I'm sorry, but I can't," Jon tried to refuse politely.

"Oh, Jon you haven't changed, you're still too busy working to have some fun and enjoy a beautiful day. Now, we are not taking no as an answer." She tugged at his arm and she wrapped her fingers around his.

Jon didn't want to make a scene so he seceded. He turned towards Mindy and Alicia, "I'll be back later," he said in a stoic voice as he walked away with the three drop dead gorgeous models.

"Who the hell do you think that is?" Mindy whispered.

Alicia's moment of surprise and passed and now the only thing she felt was abhorrence and jealousy. Still trying to control her disgust she clenched her teeth, "His ex," she replied.

For the rest of the evening Alicia was unable to concentrate. Her chest felt compressed and her stomach had a pain in its pit. Every five minute she checked the time. This had been the longest day so far.

Jon never returned before the Show closed. As Mindy and Alicia walked back to the hotel, self doubt started to creep into Alicia's mind. *Why would he choose me over her? She's beautiful, rich and probably well educated. I have nothing to offer. I'm a homeless, uneducated broke girl from the wrong side of town.*

Mindy put the key into the door of their room and asked as she opened the door, "Are you going to go for a swim, or are you going to take a dive into Mr. Anonymous?"

All Alicia wanted to do was climb into bed, watch television, and sulk. "I think I'll stay in tonight. I'm kind of tired."

As they entered the room they were met by the aroma of roses. There on their table sat a large bouquet of red roses, with an envelope inserted in the card holder. Mindy jumped with joy as she reached for the envelope. "Oh honey, looks like someone has the hots for you!"

"What makes you think they're for me?" Alicia said with disbelief. She walked slowly towards the enormous arrangement.

Mindy took the envelope and handed it to Alicia, "Here you open it!"

Alicia took the envelope and reached in. She pulled out a hand written note and two gift cards:

*Alicia and Mindy,*

*I'm sorry I had to leave so abruptly. I know I said I would be back, but I was unable to get away. The good news is I sold Katrina on the Queen Antoinette Dress. Please enjoy an evening at the Spa, you two deserve it!*

*Sincerely, Jon Whit*

"Are you serious? He sold the most expensive dress it the store line, each dress is well over $5,000! Boy, he's good, and gracious!" Mindy grabbed her card and danced all the way to the bathroom. "We'll leave as soon as I get out of this stuffy suit."

Alicia was more confused than ever. *I wonder what he had to do to sell that dress, why the flowers? What is he feeling guilty about?* The more she stared at the beautiful red roses, the more her anger subsided. *He sent flowers and an evening at the spa.* She smiled and changed.

Mindy and Alicia had the works done at the spa, mud bath, a facial, steam bath, and a full body massage. They had a blast. Afterwards, Mindy was in such a good mood she decided to head to the bar, for some extra fun. Alicia decided to call it a night.

When she reached her room, she opened her purse to take out the key. She saw the suite key card. She was in such a good mood, that she wanted to thank Jon for the flowers and the spa treatment. She headed up to the suite.

******

Jon had just stepped out of the shower after his workout at the gym, when he heard a knock on the door. *Why is she knocking, I gave her a key?* He walked over to the door and opened it with a huge smile on his face. "Hello!"

"Hi baby! I thought you might be mad, that I came up without an invitation!" Janet threw her arms around Jon's neck. "I haven't been able to get you out of my mind since lunch. You know, I've missed you." She pressed her lips on his and gave him a passionate kiss.

The door was still open when Alicia arrived. She found Janet wrapped around Jon. Everything inside her began to convulse.

Jon put his hands on Janet's hips and pushed her off. "Janet, please…"

Alicia didn't care to hear the rest of that sentence. "Mr. Whit."

Quickly, Janet turned to face Alicia. She had a look on her face that said she wanted to cause her harm. "Who are you?"

Alicia was by no means threatened. She had slept on the streets for six months and had dealt with bigger and meaner bitches on the streets. If it was ghetto this slut wanted, then that is what she would get. "I'm Alicia the Assistant Manager of the Newport Beach Shop, and you are?"

Jon stepped in before the claws came out. "This is Janet Jones. She was a model at one of the dress shoots."

Janet laughed, "I think I'm more than a model at a shoot, dear. You slept with me for six months after the shoot." She ran her fingers though his hair.

Jon crabbed her hand, and pulled it way. "We broke up after that Janet."

"Then why did you greet me with such a large smile just a few minutes ago?" Janet asked in a sensual tone.

Alicia's heart dropped at the sound of those words. She couldn't take Janet's advanced anymore. She turned to Jon and in a cold tone said, "Mr. Whit, I'm sorry for interrupting. There is obviously unfinished business here. So, we can go over the leads of today in the morning." She turned and walked away. The anger had turned into sorrow once more. She took the elevator down to her room and she collapsed on top of her bed. The tears ran down her cheeks. A feeling of self doubt and unworthiness came over her. *If he didn't want her anymore, then why the smile?*

****** 

Jon didn't know what to say as Alicia walked off. Angrily he turned to Janet. He clenched his fits. "The reason I haven't called you in a year, is because I want nothing to do with you! Now, get out of my suite before I throw you out!" He pointed to the door.

"But you greeted me with a smile. I thought…"

Jon's eye flamed with rage. "I didn't know it was you on the other side of the door. Had I known you where coming up, I would have asked security to escort you back down. You and I were a mistake, one that I will never commit again. You are a shallow, conceited and a cold hearted bitch! Now leave before I…" Jon took a breath to control his temper.

Janet was shaken by the look of fury in Jon's eyes. She had never seen him this upset. He had never talked to her in that tone. She was confuse and insulted. She stepped back into the hall way and heard the door slam behind her. Her ego had been bruised. She would never forgive Jon for that.

****** 

Jon was still fuming. He ran his fingers through his hair as he paced back and forth in the living room. He took a deep breath. *I have to fix this.* He headed out of the suite and into the elevator. When he arrived at Alicia's room he knocked, but no one answered. "Alicia, open the door," he demanded.

Alicia jumped out of bed. She was still dress, but her eyes were swollen from crying. She walked to the door, but did not open it. She looked in the peep hole. Jon was standing on the other side of the door.

Jon slammed his hand on the door once more. "I'm not leaving until we talk. So if I have to stand here all night and make scene, I will."

Alicia could hear the Jon's determination. *I'll just tell him to get lost, that he should head back to his tall slutty friend.* She sighed and opened the door.

Jon waited to see who answered. When he saw Alicia, he wrapped his arm around her waist and closed the door with his other hand. He kissed her as passionately as he could and took his loose hand and placed it on the back of her head.

Alicia was overwhelmed. She had not expected Jon to overpower her. Her brain told her to push him away, to tell him to get out and to never talk to her again, but her body betrayed her. She wrapped her arms around his neck and ran her fingers through his short hair.

Once Jon could feel that Alicia had reciprocated his passion, he pressed up against her so she could feel the bulge in his pants. She moaned softly in approval. Jon moved is hand down from her head to the middle of her back. He pulled away from her lips and began to kiss her neck toward her earlobe. "Alicia, you are the only woman that I want babe."

He nibbled on her ear and whispered, "That smile was meant for you, and only you. I left the show because I didn't want to cause a scene, that's all."

Alicia wanted to tell him how angry and hurt she felt, but down deep in her heart she believed him, and forgave him. Even if she would have wanted to talk her body would not let her. It was electrified, and the space between her legs throbbed to be filled.

Jon pulled away quickly, "Alicia, where is your phone?" He looked around the room. "Where is it?"

Alicia was still in a daze. "Why?"

Jon spotted her purse by the bouquet of roses. He let her go, opened her purse, and pulled out her phone.

"Jon, what are you doing?" Alicia asked confused.

"I'm texting Mindy," he replied as his fingers quickly moved across the letters. *I'm entertaining in our room tonight. Please find somewhere to crash.*

By the time Alicia was able to move her legs again, Jon had already sent the message. "What did you do?" she uttered.

Jon showed her the text, with a grin on his face.

Alicia was about to argue when a text message came through. *That's fine I've already made other arrangements for tonight. I'll be with Billy in room 3045. Don't let the bed bugs bite ;)*

"There, now where were we?" Jon wrapped his arms around Alicia and began to kiss her neck.

The fresh scent of colon was hypnotizing. She closed her eyes and bent her head back so that Jon could kiss the bottom of her chin. "You shouldn't have sent that message. What if Mindy ends up roaming the street?"

Jon moaned has he reached down to squeeze her firm ass. "I doubt Mindy will have a hard time find a guy to take her in."

Alicia giggled and shook her head and she ran her fingers though Jon's back, "You're, bad."

"You haven't seen how bad I can be." Jon crooned in a gruff voice. He picked Alicia up and gently placed her is the center of the bed.

Alicia lay down, face up, and looked into Jon's beautiful hazel eyes. His gazed sent a second jolt of electricity through her entire body. As he reached up under her dress, she moaned with anticipation. She could feel his soft but strong hands reach for her panties. He removed her panties with such ease that it made Alicia wonder how often he gotten to practice. Jon pulled her dress up to expose her bottom half. He moaned and smiled.

Alicia sat up on the bed and pulled her dress down. She had always been self conscious about her body. She began to pull Jon's polo shirt off him. He helped by lifting up his hands. He threw his shirt on the floor. Then he reached for Alicia's dress and pulled it off over her head. Jon ran his fingers down her shoulders and then her back. He snapped her bra and exposed those prefect little nipples that peeked from behind her long hair.

Jon climbed off the bed and stood there taking in the view. "Alicia, you are so beautiful. I could stand here and stare at you all night."

Alicia blushed, turned away and reached for the bed sheets. Before she realized that she had mooned Jon, he grabbed her bottom and thrust his bulging jeans put against her. "Mmm," he groaned. He ran a finger along the soft skin between her legs. He used his finger to see how much she wanted him. "May I come in?" he asked. He flipped her on her back and stripped.

Alicia lost all self control when Jon had grabbed her ass and ran his finger in her, her inside had began to convulse, now on her back again her heart was racing. She watched as Jon removed his jeans and boxers. Jon spread her legs and began to run his tongue between her legs. As he sucked, Alicia grabbed the sheets, her breathing was erratic. She wanted him in her. She was ready to explode. "Please, Jon. Please!" she begged.

Jon gave her a grin and teased her "What, would you like?" he asked as he circled her nub with his finger.

"I want you in me. Please," she sighed and arched her back towards him.

Jon couldn't say no to Alicia. He quickly bent over the edge of the bed and grabbed his wallet. He tore open a condom and put it in place. He tossed the wallet on the floor. Alicia quickly wrapped her legs around him and directed him towards her. Jon wanted to take his time as he made his way in, but Alicia wasn't going to wait. As soon as she felt him at her opening she used her legs to pull him all the way in.

Jon had not expected Alicia to have such strong legs. "Hey, that's not fair."

"Why don't you come down here and make a personal complaint," Alicia teased and she bit her bottom lip.

Jon placed his hands on either side of Alicia's head. He bent over, kissed her and moaned, "I like the way you twitch."

As Jon began to sway in and out, Alicia's body exploded in ecstasy. She arched her back and moaned with pleasure. She loved the way he made her body feel. Her body went limp, and for a second she forgot how to breathe. *I don't want this to ever end.*

Jon loved watching Alicia climax. It aroused him more than he could explain. *Oh she's perfect.* Soon, his breathing became erratic and he could no longer hold back. He gave out a rough growl and his body began to twitch. He collapsed on top of Alicia.

It was around three in the morning when Jon noticed that Alicia was wrapped around his body asleep. His heart filled with a warmth and calmness he had never felt before. *I could get use to this.* He wished he could spend the rest of his life waking up to this beautiful golden face. Jon whispered and ran his finger over her face. "Alicia, honey."

Alicia opened her eyes slowly. "Hum."

"I think I should go now," Jon said as he kissed her head.

Alicia shook her head. "Don't leave," she pleaded.

"But Mindy might come back. You said you didn't want her to know." He said in a quiet voice.

"Jon, please don't leave me." She mumbled half asleep. She snuggled closer to him and continued to dream.

Jon smiled and closed his eyes. "Okay, baby. I'll stay as long as you want."

# Chapter 8: The Day After

Mindy carefully opened the door to her room at eight in the morning. She hoped Alicia and the mystery man would be gone. She peeked in and saw the beds were empty, but she could hear giggling and running water in the shower. She tiptoed over to the closet, grabbed her suit and changed as quickly as she could. She couldn't make out what was being said, but she could hear Alicia's giggles and laughter.

Mindy was happy to hear her having fun. Alicia never got out much and Mindy worried that her best friend my end up alone forever.

When she was dressed, she sat at the edge of her bed to slip on her heels. There on the floor sat an open wallet with a man's driver's license. Her jaw dropped and her eyes popped open as she read the name, "Jon Whit, oh my God!" She jumped up off the bed and ran out the door making sure not to slam it on the way out.

Alicia had dried and wrapped a towel around her body. "Jon we need to talk." She knew that sooner or later, he would be leaving and she needed to know what to expect when he did. She didn't want to invest any more of herself in a relationship that was merely a fling.

Jon wrapped his arms around her, "Okay, but can we do it this evening? I need to go and change into my suit."

"But Jon, I have to go home this evening. It's Sunday," Alicia tried not to pout.

Jon gave her a warm hug, and took a whiff of her hair. "Tell Mindy that you plan to stay longer and that your boyfriend will take you home later this evening."

Alicia couldn't believe what she heard. "My what?"

Jon kissed her neck, "You don't want me as your boyfriend?"

"Of course I do, but you're leaving soon."Alicia relinquished.

"Then that settles it. I'll be your boyfriend and you'll be my girlfriend." He smiled as he said it. "Now, tell Mindy you're staying and we'll continue this conversation later." He kissed her on the head and headed towards the door. "I might be late to the show this morning, I hope you won't mind."

Alicia finished dressing and wondered when Mindy would arrive to change. She finally gave up waiting and headed to the Convention Hall. Mindy was already there.

Alicia asked with surprise and apprehension, "How did you change into your suit?"

Mindy fiddled with some business cards in her hand. "I snuck in while you were in the shower, but I didn't see anything." She could not bring herself to look at Alicia.

Alicia took in a deep breath, "You know!"

"I didn't mean to snoop, but his wallet was on the floor with his driver's license just there. When I bent down to put on my heels," Mindy looked remorseful.

Alicia was dumbfounded. She felt a cold wave travel through her body. She didn't know what to say. "I'm sorry, I didn't tell you sooner, but I just couldn't." She lowered her head in shame.

Mindy wrapped an arm around Alicia. "I'm just happy to see you're having fun, even if you are playing with fire."

Alicia signed, "I know, that's why don't want anyone to find out."

The doors to the Bridal Show opened and women started pouring in. Another busy day was ahead.

******

It was noon by the time Jon showed up. "Hi ladies, sorry I couldn't be here this morning, but I had phone calls to return. Please go to lunch, and I'll stay here."

Alicia and Mindy walked to their new favorite Convention Center deli. Tired of eating healthy all weekend they decided to have some fun. They order a large Panini each instead and sat down at their usual table.

"OMG, Alicia you're banging the Prez!" Mindy blurted and she sat down.

Alicia just shook her head. "Mindy please, not so loud." She looked around to make sure no one had her.

"I'm sorry, but I just can't believe it! You must have wasted him out last night if he couldn't get up and make it this morning." She played with her tea. "So, now what's going to happen, the show is over?"

Alicia had a worried look on her face. "I don't know. He asked me to stay here with him this evening so we could talk. So, I plan to stay and see what happens. And…" she stopped herself before she said too much.

"And what?" Mindy watched her intensely.

"And he asked me to be his girlfriend." Alicia ran her hand through her hair trying to clam herself.

"He, what!" Mindy yelled. "You've got to be kidding me! Who asks that anymore? You mean he wants you to be exclusive?" Mindy looked like she was about to pass out.

"Please Mindy, calm down and lower your voice." Alicia tried to not blush but Mindy was making it hard.

"Well, what did you say?" Mindy blurted.

"I said yes, but we still need to talk about what that means," Alicia wringed her hands.

Mindy leaned close and whispered, "Oh man, when I told you to go out and have fun, I didn't think you'd screw our boss! Dam, girl you've got some balls!"

They both busted up laughing. Alicia shook her head. "That's why I love you besty, you're crude, but you make me laugh! So tell me, where were you all night?"

They finished eating their lunch while Mindy describe her one night stand. Mindy had no trouble talking about her sex life openly. Most of the time Alicia just blushed as Mindy described every little detail of her evening.

The show ended at four. Mark walked into the hall pulling the dolly behind him. "Hi ladies! How did it go?"

"Exhausting!" Mindy sighed as she leaned against the table.

Jon looked at the tiredness on her face, and felt guilty about kicking her out of her own room. "Mindy, why don't you and Alicia go back to the room and rest before you head home."

Mindy looked at Jon, with an incredulous look. "But, there is still so much to put away!"

"I think that I can handle taking down this booth, besides Mr. Stone is here to help." Jon turned a looked at Mark for support.

"Sure thing." Mark started to take the dresses off the mannequins and piling them up on the table. There were very few catalogues and post cards left so the only thing left to do was to break down the booth.

Mindy looked at Alicia. "Okay, then we'll head up and pack. Thank you, Mr. Whit. Will we see you tomorrow?"

Jon smiled, "Yes, I'll be in the shop tomorrow. Have a good evening."

Alicia and Mindy walked away together. Jon stood and watched as Alicia walked away shaking bottom from side to side. A huge grin spread over his face.

"Isn't that just the sweetest sight?" Mark remarked as he drooled.

"Yes, it certainly is." Jon agreed, but at the same time twinged at the thought that this man was drooling over his woman.

******

Mindy and Alicia finished packing. They had their luggage delivered to the front door. "Okay Alicia, I'm going to leave you here to sort out this delicious mess you have gotten yourself into. Please call me and let me know what happens." Mindy gave Alicia a hug. "See you sweetie."

Alicia left her luggage in the storage room and went back up to the suite. She walked in and felt out of place. Her eye quickly honed in on the splendid view of the city. She felt drawn to the window. She placed her right hand on her left arm, as she stood there alone. She sighed.

Jon walked in and found her staring out the window. "Hi babe, what are you doing?"

Alicia turned and looked at him. I was just standing here admiring the view." She turned back to stare out the window some more. "I can't believe I'm here, never in my wildest dreams could I have imagined that one day I would be in a suite overseeing this spectacular view." A tear ran down her cheek.

Jon wrapped his arms around her as he joined her by the window. He leaned in, "What's making you sad?" He whispered.

Alicia quickly brushed off the tear and coaxed a smile on her face. "Nothing, I'm just being silly."

Jon was not about to let her off the hook just yet. He held his grip around her waist. "As your boyfriend I want to know everything about you. I mean, I already know how beautiful you are, but I also want to know what makes you tick. Please tell me."

Alicia stared out the window, and took a moment to think. She knew that if she expected Jon to be honest with her, she would need to be just as honest with him. "I was just remembering when I left home," she mumbled.

"You left home?" Jon repeated hoping there was more to this story.

She continued reminiscing. She told Jon about the night she left home at age 17 never to return. Living on the streets had not been easy, but living with her father, a devout religious man who ruled him home with an iron hand had been harder. Her mother was a servant to her father and had no voice in the house. Alicia never wanted to end up like her. That is why she had left. She would always be thankful to all her high school friends who let her crash on their sofa until graduation. But, she would always be in debt to her friend Melinda who had gotten her a position in sales for one of those cell phone companies. While, she had no formal education, she was a willing learner. She became very good at selling. She had no choice, it was sell or starve.

Jon listened and did not interrupt. Now he understood why she said she had no family. "How did you end up working in the bridal industry?"

"After a few years of selling phones, I met Mindy. She had come into the store looking for a new phone. So I sold her one. She was so impressed with my ability to sell that she offered me a job as a Bridal Consultant. She said that the commissions where better than I was making, and there was a possibility to move up in the company. I have always wanted to have my own store, and the phone company is a 'good old boys club.' There was no way they would give me a store over a man. So I took a job working in Mindy's store." Alicia smiled and turned to meet Jon's eyes. "And, I've loved my job ever since."

Jon smiled and kissed her. "Thank you for letting me in."

Alicia turned and looked at him with serious eyes. "Jon we need to talk. I need to know what's going to happen. I can't stay here. I have to go home, and you have to go back to Michigan soon."

Jon spoke with sincerity in his voice and vulnerability in his gaze, "Alicia, you make me feel alive. Every time I look at you I can't focus on anything else. I have never felt like this. I don't know what will happen after I leave, but I know that I don't want be without you."

Alicia smiled. She couldn't ask for anymore than that. She hadn't felt this strongly about a man ever. All she wanted to know was that he wanted her, and he did. That is all that mattered for now. "But, Jon what's going to happen at work? I don't want to lose my new position as Assistant Manager because I'm seeing the President."

Jon took a moment to think. "Ms. Garcia, I promise that in the work area I will keep my hands to myself and be as professional as I can be. Trust me, I've been known to be a work-alcoholic. So keeping focus on business shouldn't be a problem."

Alicia took Jon's earlobe between her fingers, and began to rub softly, "Okay, I can live with that."

"But Alicia, after hours, your mine," Jon leaned down and grabbed her bottom lip with his and began to suck.

Alicia was taken by surprise, but did not pull away, she couldn't. Jon had an invisible hold on her that she didn't understand.

Jon had managed to move his hand under she t-shirt and snapped her bra in less than five seconds. Now he was fondling her perfectly round breast. Feeling himself more aroused, he picked Alicia up off the floor. She wrapped her legs around his torso. Jon turned and walked into the bed.

\*\*\*\*\*\*

"Jon, it's almost seven," she said as she sat up on the king size bed with the sheets wrapped around her bare breast. "Please take me home. I have to open the shop tomorrow."

Jon laid his head on her lap rubbing his lips between her legs, with only a sheet preventing him from what he truly wanted. "Why don't you call Mindy and tell her you'll be in later."

While it was tempting, she was not about to lose sight of what needed to be done. "Monday is her day off. I have to open."

"Can I spend the night at your place, then?" Jon asked hopeful.

"If I let you spend the night, you and I both know we wouldn't get very much sleep," Alicia giggled.

Jon sat up, "I can't help it, you drive me wild." He placed a soft kiss on her lower lip. "Can we at least get dinner, I'm starving."

\*\*\*\*\*\*

Jon found a nice restaurant by Alicia's apartment. As they drove to dinner Alicia asked, "Jon, do you like being the President of 'From this Day Forward?'"

Jon gave her a one sided smile. "I love my work. I enjoy making money and closing deals. I truly do, but work is a beast that takes over your life, if you let it." He paused for a moment, then continued, "Sometimes, I wish I wasn't the President. I see how happy my brother is with his life and part of me is jealous. He has something else to come home to, not just work."

He laughed, "My mom is worried, I'm going it die alone. She is always trying to convince me to let her set me up with one of her friend's daughters. I know she means well, but it can get annoying."

"Well, now you can tell her you have a girlfriend, and maybe she'll ease up on you." Alicia stroked her hand over his.

Jon couldn't believe how warm those words had made him feel. His heart melted. "That's right! I now have the most beautiful girlfriend a man could ever wish for."

Alicia blushed. "Now, you're just trying to get into my pants."

Jon laughed, but he knew he truly meant it. "We're here let eat."

The Italian Restaurant was fancier than Alicia had expected and she felt underdressed in her old jeans and t-shirt. Jon didn't seem to mind what she wore, so that made her feel better. Dinner went without incident. Alicia order tea and Jon had wine. Alicia asked about life in Michigan. He told her about growing up with an annoying baby brother and traveling with his parents to different states during their summer vacations. He spoke kindly of his mom with warmth in his voice as he described how she would spend time with them while his father worked. He spoke of his dad with admiration, of how he managed to balance the love for his mother and kid with a demanding job.

The more Alicia learned about Jon, the more she loved him. She wanted to be with him forever, and be his distraction from work, but deep down she knew that it was impossible. For now she would enjoy his presence, and when he was gone, she'd find a way to deal with the loss.

# Chapter 9: The Surprise

Monday morning Alicia arrived to work in her 2000 Black Prizm. She wanted to be the first there. Her car raddled and hissed down the street so badly that she was afraid she would get pulled over for noise pollution. She still needed to save some more before she could buy a newer model, and she was embarrassed to be seen in this old piece of junk now that she was in management. Her dream car was on her goal poster, but for now she would settle for anything that didn't announce her arrival a block in advance.

She opened the shop and soon she greeted all the bridal consultants. As a group they headed for the goal wall and they took a moment to check their goals. Then, they stood in a circle and took turns taking out customer objections from a can. Each consultant thought of a way to respond to an objection and make the bride feel more at ease. After that they all went to work.

Soon the shop was full of women looking for dresses. The appointments from the show had started to show up. The shop was full of happy buzzing when Jon showed up a few hours later. Alicia was in the back office entering the leads from the Bridal Show into their contact list and newsletter list on the computer.

Chloe came into the office, "Alicia, Mr. Whit is here to see you." She moved to the side to let him in.

Alicia jumped out of her seat. "Mr. Whit, how are you?" She shook his hand. "I see you met Chloe McAlan, she's one of the best consultants here at Newport."

Chloe blushed and shrugged her shoulders. "Alicia is too kind. She's the one who is amazing. She knows how to bring out the best in all of us. And her ideas on improving our store have definitely made a positive impact."

"Well, I'm glad to hear that everyone here has such high regards for each other. It's nice to come into a store with such a warm atmosphere," Jon smiled at both.

Chloe's infatuation with Jon was quite obvious. She couldn't stop staring at him. She stood there smiling for a long moment.

"Thank you Chloe for showing Mr. Whit into the office," Alicia tried to break her spell.

Chloe turned to look at Alicia and realized that she had been staring. She blushed and said, "Oh, yes. I have another bride coming soon." She turned to walk out of the office, then she remembered, "Oh Alicia, I think we are running low on coffee. Do you want me to head on over to the coffee shop to pick some up?"

"No need Chloe. I'll pick some up when I go exchange business cards." Alicia smiled.

Jon sat in the chair in front of the desk. Alicia leaned back into the desk. "So Ms. Garcia, what are you working on today?" Jon was having a hard time keeping a straight face.

Alicia just gave him the 'don't you dare start' look. "This morning, I am planning on entering all of the leads into the computer. Then this afternoon I plan to network with the businesses in the shopping strip. Hopefully we can help each other by bring in clients. We'll offer them flyers for our dresses, and we'll offer our brides tanning services, bands, spa service."

"Sounds good, I'll just sit over here on this table and set up my portable office. Once you are done entering the leads, I'll join you for your networking trip."

The day went as planned. Jon and Alicia spent the afternoon networking. Jon was quite impressed by the way Alicia was able to network with the businesses around the shop. He was truly pleased and amazed with her people skills. She had an uncanny demeanor which people found nonthreatening. He was glad she was working for their company and not their competitors.

The shop had closed for the evening. Alicia's feet where throbbing in those uncomfortable heels. She tried not to limp her way towards her car. She didn't want Jon to see her in pain.

"Where would you like to go to dinner?" Jon asked as they walk towards Alicia's car. He tried to pretend he did not see Alicia flinch as she walked in those shoes.

Alicia was not use to going out so much. She missed sitting around her home and eating a home cooked meal. "Jon, I really am not in the mood to go out to dinner. Would you mind if I cooked dinner for you instead. I'll stop by the market and pick up a few items before heading over to my place."

Jon frowned for a second. He had been holding back all day and wanted to desperately to tell Alicia his news. Quickly he came up with a plan. "What if we take my car and stop by the market. Then, we can head over to your place together."

They arrived at Alicia's clunker. "I can't leave my car here. It'll get towed. What if I drive home and then we go to the market together." She didn't understand why he wanted to go with her to the market, but she wasn't in the mood to argue.

Jon looked at Alicia's Prizm. He couldn't believe this thing actually ran. He stood there and watched as she opened the door and started the car. "Okay. I'll follow you."

Alicia gave him a smile, waved and drove off. The car bounced and rattled so much it made Jon laugh. He shook his head and walked back to his rented Acura.

When Alicia had parked in the car port, Jon pulled up behind her. "Hop in, I'm driving to the market."

Alicia opened the door and stepped in. "The market is just around the corner, we can walk."

"No, I don't think your feet are up for walking in those heels anymore," Jon responded knowing all to well that they were not headed back to her place just yet.

Alicia was tired of being in heels, so she sat down in the passenger's seat and slipped out of her pumps. *I wish I would have brought my flats before getting in the car.*

In the market each went their separate ways. Alicia went shopping for dinner and Jon picked up some breakfast items. They met at the register. Jon insisted on paying for everything, but Alicia was unsure why he had breakfast in the cart. She hoped he didn't plan to spend the night at her place.

Once the groceries were in the car, Jon drove in the opposite direction. Alicia was perplexed. "Jon, where are you going? My place is in the other direction."

Jon tried to play it cool. "I know, but there is something I've wanted to show you all day. It will only take a few minutes. I promise." He turned and gave Alicia a mischievous grin.

Alicia simply shook her head. The power Jon's smile had over her was incomprehensible. She sat back and took her shoes once more.

Jon drove past the Bridal Shop. A few more blocks down, he turned on to a street the over looked the beach. He drove up into a car port and parked. "We're here," he announced as he jumped out of the car and ran to open Alicia's door.

Alicia looked out the window all she saw where luxury town homes overlooking the beach.

"Where exactly are we?" she questioned as she stepped out of the car.

Jon took Alicia by the hand and walked her to the front door of the townhome. He took the key out of his pocket, and opened the door. Alicia followed him with a confused look. "Jon, what is this?"

"This is where I'll be staying for the next few weeks," Jon said as he pressed a button by the front door.

The curtains facing the ocean opened up and Alicia had a perfect view of the beach and the setting sun. "Look, the terrace has a small table and two chairs so that we could sit and listen to the waves as they crash on the beach, and we can watch the sunset." Jon said with a smile that went from ear to ear.

Alicia looked around the place, it had a small kitchen, a beautiful living room with a large comfortable sofa and a flat screen television. The place had a warm homely feeling. She smiled, "It's nice."

"Will this kitchen do?" he walked into the kitchen, and turned on the lights.

"Yes, it will do." Alicia was not such what Jon meant, but he was beaming and she didn't want to burst his bubble.

"Should I go to the car and get the groceries?" he asked as he headed for the car.

"Jon, I …" Alicia didn't want to upset Jon, but she really didn't want to spend her evening in her stuffy suit and heels. She just wanted to go home, change and snuggle on her sofa.

Jon stopped at the door, and looked at her. He put his hand on the door knob and said, "Oh babe, I forgot to tell you, go though those doors, there's a gift for you through there."

Alicia sighed. She placed her purse on the living room coffee table and walked into the bed room. It was a lagre beautifully decorated room. On the king size bed there was a red silk halter top dress and a pair of expensive sandals. *It's beautiful!* She quickly slipped out of her heels and changed into the halter top dress. It fit perfectly. She looked in the mirror to check out how it looked. She wasn't vain, but this dress made her look fabulous.

Jon was unpacking the groceries, when Alicia walked into the living room. He turned and saw her stroll in. "Wow, you look stunning!"

"Thank you," she said as she spun around for Jon to get a good view of all of her. "The dress is stunning, and the sandals are very comfortable, but you shouldn't have."

Jon walked towards her pulled in by her beauty. He wrapped his arms around her, and looked into her deep honey eyes. Standing only a fraction of a centimeter way from her lips he said, "If you don't like it, I can take it back."

"No. I do love it, but it's too expensive. I don't want you to spend so much money on me." Alicia could almost taste his lips.

Jon finally leaned in and kissed her gently. "I really liked this dress, and I want you to have it. Please, accept it."

Alicia simply murmured, "Thank you, how did you know it would fit?"

"I had some help from the girl that works at the dress shop. She said this one would fit, and I'm glad she was right." He leaned in for another kiss.

"How about we skip dinner and we just start with desert." He leaned in and licked his lips with a teasing sparkle in his eyes.

Alicia laughed and pushed him away. "How about I go to the kitchen and prepare those tostadas first?"

Jon pouted, but let her go. "Okay, I guess I can wait for desert. What would you like me to help with?"

Alicia had never heard a man ask to help in the kitchen. When she lived at home it was her mother's job to take care of dinner. "I can handle making tostadas. It's not that difficult. Why don't you sit on the terrace and enjoy the view." She leaned her head towards the sliding door.

"But, I would rather stare at the view in here." Jon gave her a one sided grin.

Alicia's phone rang. She picked up her purse and took out the phone. She looked at it without answering. "It's Mindy," she wasn't sure what to say to her friend. She stood there thinking.

Jon noticed the hesitation in her. "Tell her you are spending the night here with me," he noticed he had made it sound like an order. Quickly he tried to recover. "If it's okay with you."

Alicia didn't plan to stay all night. "But, I don't have anything to wear," she said realizing that she probably wouldn't need anything from the mischievous smile Jon was giving her.

"Would you like me to text her for you?" Jon volunteered.

# Chapter 10: Dinner For Two

"No I'll call her, after dinner and let her know." She took the phone into the kitchen, and started to look for the can opener.

Jon started to follow her when his phone rang. He looked to see who was calling. "Alicia, I have to take this. I'll be outside."

Alicia nodded as she opened the can of bean. She preferred eating home cooked beans, but she was never in the mood to cook a whole pot just for herself. She placed them in a small pot and set the stove on low. While the beans warmed, she chopped the tomatoes and cilantro. She thinly sliced the cabbage and shredded the cheese. Now that everything was ready, she went into the living room and turned on the radio to her favorite radio station. An upbeat Cumbia song played as she bounced into the kitchen and started put the tostadas together.

******

"Hey little bro, what's up?" Jon asked as he sat down on the terrace chair overlooking the beach.

"Not much. What's going on with you?" responded the voice on the other end of the phone.

"Not much, why?" Jon replied.

"Mom called me concerned, and wanted me to check up on you. She says you've decided to move to LA. Is that true?"

Jon smirked and watched the blue waves crash into the sand. "You know mom, she's always so dramatic. I've decided to stay in LA for a few weeks. The weather here is great. Right now, I'm sitting on the terrace overseen the sunset. While I'm here I plan to visit all the local shops and I plan go to the Bridal

Fashion Show and see what's happening here in the West Coast."

There was a moment of silence on the phone. "Jon, you sound too up beat. Usually you sound tired, and stressed out. So tell me the truth, what's really going on? If I can't report back to mom with a satisfactory answer, she's just going to get on a plane and show up at your door."

Jon tilted his head back and laughed. "Okay, if you must know I've met someone. So tell mom I'm working on those grand kids for her. That should keep her out of my way for a while."

"Well now, that sounds more like it. That would explain the sudden interest in your Western Shops. So, how hot is she? I mean, how tall blond and gorgeous is she?"

"She's nothing like that at all. Well she is gorgeous, but she's petite, naturally tan, long burnet hair with honey eyes and a smile that makes your heart stop. She's funny, dedicated to her job, with Latin fire in her soul, and quite charming." Jon's heart skipped a beat just thinking about her.

"Sounds like you're falling hard for her. Just be careful, bro. I don't want to see you heartbroken."

"I'll do my best to keep my head on straight." Jon tried to reassure him. "Now hang up and call mom. I'm such she's dying to know what's gotten into me."

"I think you'd better email me a photo or else I doubt she's going to buy the girl story."

"Okay, I'll go in and take a picture right now." Jon stood up and opened the glass doors."

"Is that music in the background?"

"Yea, that's Latin music. Alicia loves that stuff. Okay bro, hugs and kisses to the kids and the wife." Jon stood in the living room watching Alicia move and serve the plates. He thought that he could definitely see himself living with this woman for the rest of his life.

She walked into the living room caring two plates filled with tostadas. Even with her hands full she managed to keep the beat of the music. Shoulders rotating, hips swaying and a smile that could make the North Pole melt. "Hey, can you bring the glasses out to the terrace."

Jon quickly ran into the kitchen and picked up the glasses along with the napkins. Alicia stood by the sliding door waiting for Jon to open the door. They stepped outside and Alicia placed the plates down. "I hope you like these. I mean they're not gourmet food, but it's homey."

Jon placed the glasses on the table. "They look delicious."

Alicia sat across from Jon. She watched as Jon grabbed a tostada and took a bite.

"These are pretty good." Jon said sincerely and he licked his lips.

Alicia smiled and picked a tostada up and took a bite. "These are okay, but they would be better if I had cooked the bean from scratch."

"Did you want me to go and buy some beans so you can cook them?" Jon asked.

Alicia covered her mouth and laughed, "No, cooking beans is a four hour endeavor, and I don't want to have tostadas for breakfast. Besides I haven't cooked beans in years. I don't think I remember how."

"If you change your mind, just let me know and I go out and get them for you," Jon offered as he took another bite. The tostada fell apart and landed all over his plate.

"I think I did something wrong. My dinner broke." He looked at the mess on his plate.

Alicia laughed, "I forgot to tell you to hold the tostada from the bottom. Now, you'll have to eat it with a fork or use the tostada as chips and scoop it up. I'm guessing this is the first time you've eaten tostadas."

"Yes, it is. Let's just say I haven't had much exposure to Latin food." Jon tried his best to scoop up his food.

"Oh man, I almost forgot." He pulled out his phone for his pocket. "Smile," he said as he snapped a picture.

"What are you doing?" Alicia asked a little disoriented.

"Stevie wants a picture. He didn't believe me when I told him I had a beautiful woman as my girlfriend. So I promised to take a picture and send it to him."

"I'm sorry, who's Stevie," she asked still confused.

"My brother Steven," Jon clarified as he emailed the picture.

"So your brother is going to believe you if you send him a picture of me? How does he know you didn't just take a random picture of a girl walking by? I think the best way to prove that we are together is to take a couples picture." She said and she took a drink from her tea.

"Okay," Jon walked over to her side of the table and kneeled down next to her, then with one hand held the camera out in front of them he leaned in closer to Alicia. "Ready? Smile!" just before he snapped the picture he turned and kissed her on the cheek.

Alicia couldn't believe he had done that. "Jon, you can't send that photo to your brother!"

"I already did," he said and he hit the send button.

"Jon, you really shouldn't have. What is your brother and his wife going to think of me?"

"They'll think you're gorgeous." Jon tried to assure her.

"They'll think I'm easy!" Alicia murmured and frowned.

"Nonsense, besides who cares what they think! All I care is to let them know how happy..." Jon voice tapered off. He told his brother he would try to keep is head straight, but she was making it difficult. He wanted to say, *How happy you make me feel,* but instead he said, "we are."

Alicia didn't know what to respond. She didn't want to make a bad impression with Jon's family. Although she didn't know where this relationship was headed, she found herself thinking of a future together.

The sun had set and now only the sound of the waves could be heard. Alicia shivered; the cool evening breeze was making her tremble. She rubbed her arms to warm them.

Jon stood up and took off his suit coat. "Here babe put this on and go inside. I'll clean up."

Alicia could not believe what she was hearing. *A man who also cleans! He's a keeper.* She reached for Jon's coat and put it on. "I'll help you clean up."

"No way, you made dinner now I'll clean. Please go rest. I'll wash the dishes." He kissed her on the cheek and shushed her away.

"Okay, I have to go call Mindy anyway." she acquiesced. She gave him a peck on the cheek and went inside.

"Hi Mindy, how are things?" Alicia asked as she sat down on the quite comfortable living room sofa. She used the remote to turn the sound system off.

"Good, are you coming home tonight?" responded the voice on the phone.

"I think I'll spend the night with…" She didn't know how to refer to Jon. "my boyfriend."

Jon dropped the dishes in the sink and realized he was still in his suit. He walked towards the bedroom to change before cleaning the kitchen. When he heard Alicia refer to him as his boyfriend it gave him goose bumps. He kissed her on the head as he headed past her.

Mindy laughed. "So you've decided to continue seeing Jon? It's okay, just be careful. I don't want to see you hurt, all right?"

"Okay. I guess I'll see you on tomorrow?" Alicia said as she slipped out of her sandals and placed her feet onto the sofa and under her dress.

"I doubt that. I'll see you on Wednesday at the shop. Have a nice day off tomorrow." Mindy replied.

"I already entered all the leads into the computer. So you won't have to worry about that tomorrow." Alicia leaned sideways onto the sofa's arm rest and rubbed her eyes. "So, I'll at least call you tomorrow. Bye."

"Bye, besty! Don't let the bed bugs bite." Mindy giggled as she hung up.

Alicia placed the phone on the coffee table, and closed her eyes. She hadn't realized how tried she really was. *I'll just rest for a while before I get up and help Jon with the dishes.* She wiggled to toes to release the pain from the heels and fell asleep.

When Jon returned to the living room he saw Alicia asleep on the sofa. She looked ethereal. He watched as she lay on her side with one arm under her head and the other across her chest. She held tight to his coat for warmth. He listened to her breathe in and out softly. *She's more precious than gold.* He tiptoed past her to finish cleaning the kitchen.

Alicia awoke to the sound of clicking keyboard strokes. For a moment she was disoriented. *Where am I?* Then she remembered. "Jon?"

"Yes, babe?" he looked up from behind his laptop. He was sitting in the recliner across the living room.

"I think, I'm going to bed now. Can I borrow one of your t-shirts to sleep in?" Alicia asked as she sat up and placed her feet on the floor.

"Sure. They're in the top drawer of the dresser; I've got some work to finish up, before I join you."

Alicia smiled, "Good night then." She walked into the bedroom and closed the door.

When she opened the drawer to pull out a t-shirt, there were only two items, a pink silk robe and a pink chemise. She smiled and put them back.

While they were very pretty, she liked sleeping comfortably in cotton. She opened the drawer to the right and found Jon's white t-shirts. She took her halter dress off, and opened the closet door to hang her dress up.

There in the closet she for four more dresses, all just as beautiful and expensive as the one she had in her hand. When did he go shopping? How long does he think I'm going to be here? She shrugged her shoulders, place the dress on a hanger and close the door.

When she had finally gotten comfortable in this new bed, she began to think. *What am I doing here? I can't stay here forever. Sooner or later Jon is going to leave. This is not real. This is not his home, nor his bed. It's a temporary vacation for this very busy man. I'm just a distraction for him, a momentary lapse in his hectic life. Can I afford to fall in love knowing that it's all going to end within a few days? No, I can't be distracted from my goals. Love is not what I want right now. I need to stay focused on work.* With that thought she fell asleep.

At around midnight Jon decided to call it a night. He had emailed his brother to see if he had gotten the pictures. Steven had responded, "Not bad. She is definitely not your usual type. Sara thinks she's cute, but we both agreed that we should probably not show mom the second picture you sent. We don't think mom is ready to see you kissing another woman."

Jon grinned, closed the laptop and headed to bed. He quietly opened the door so as to not wake Alicia. He stripped down to his boxers and slid into bed next to Alicia. He wanted to holder, but didn't want to wake her.

Alicia, still asleep, turned towards him and moved in closer. Jon pulled in towards her. He could feel her faint breath on his chest. Jon found the warmth her body radiated soothing. He loved the scent of her hair, the warmth and smoothness of her body. *How can I make this last?* He closed his eyes and fell into a deep sleep.

# Chapter 11: The Cat Walk

Alicia woke up before Jon. She carefully slipped out of bed and into the shower. She knew Jon was up late and didn't want to wake him. She jumped into the shower and then realizing she had no clean clothes of her own, she slipped back into the white t-shirt without any choice. The floor under her feet was cold, but she quietly slipped out into the bedroom. She left Jon sleeping and walked back into the kitchen. She was pleasantly surprised to see that Jon had done a very good job of cleaning up.

"I think I'll make scrambled eggs," she whispered to herself as she bent down to look in the refrigerator. *Oh, and I think I need some coffee.*

When Jon awoke, he felt around the bed hoping to feel Alicia's body before getting up, but she was nowhere. His senses finally awoke to the aroma of coffee. *She's already in the kitchen?* He looked at the clock on the night stand. *It's eight, too early to get up, but I'd better have some coffee, and help with breakfast.*

Jon walked into the living room following his nose, from there he could see Alicia's beautiful silhouette. Her damp hair had soaked his t-shirt causing it to cling to her breasts. The bottom of the t-shirt reached just to the edge of hips and every time she moved he could see her firm derrière. *What a sight to wake up to!* "Good morning."

"Oh, hi, I hope I didn't wake you. I was just getting breakfast ready. Would you like some eggs for breakfast?" she smiled as she turned to places the eggs on the plate.

"No, you didn't wake me. My nose made me get out of bed and follow the sweet smell of coffee, and yes scrambled eggs sound good." Jon poured himself a cup and took a sip. He leaned back on the counter to watch as Alicia finishing setting the table. Her nipples kept calling to him. The cup of coffee was the only thing keeping him from taking her right there in the kitchen.

Alicia beckoned Jon to the table with a teasing smile. "Do you plan to join me? Or are you going to just stand there and stare at my breast all morning?"

Jon blushed he didn't think he was being that obvious. "Sorry, I didn't mean to stare."

"You certainly could have fooled me." Alicia laughed as she took a sip of coffee.

Jon walked over to the table and sat across from Alicia. "Alicia, I know that today is your day off, but I was wondering if you would like to go out on a business date with me this evening."

Alicia raised her brows, "What kind of business date?"

Jon swallowed his eggs before speaking. "Well, this evening is the Summer Line Fashion Show. All the new and upcoming designers will be presenting their newest creations. Since I'm in town, I plan to go and meet with them to see if there is anyone new and exciting we can add to our personal dress line. Usually, I go alone, but I thought you might like to help me pick out something new for the coming seasons."

Alicia's asked with disbelief and surprise, "You mean I get to sit on the front row of the catwalk? And, you want me to help you look for the new designers?"

"Only if you want to," Jon replied as he continued to eat.

"Of course I want to! I've never been to a Fashion Show," she enthusiastically responded. "But, what can I wear to the show?"

Jon swallowed before speaking, "Mum, I'm going down to the Warehouse, in downtown L.A., if you'd like to come, you can pick out something to wear."

"Jon, I don't want you to think I'm not grateful, but I don't know if I can accept that offer." Alicia sipped her coffee and gave Jon an intense look.

"Why?" Jon frowned.

"I don't want to give the wrong impression. I mean, some people might think I'm simply dating you because you shower me with expensive clothes," Alicia frowned and placed her cup on the table.

"I really don't understand. What does it matter what other people think, and I don't think I'm showering you with expensive clothes." Jon sighed and sipped his coffee.

"Then what do you call all the dresses in the closet, and the night gown in the drawer? Did you buy those items for someone else?" Alicia waved her right arm towards the bedroom and placed her left palms down on the table. Her nostrils flared. She gave Jon a defiant look.

She didn't understand why her blood had begun to boil. But she was definitely irritated by Jon's indifference at her concerns.

Jon grinned, "No I bought them for you," he shrugged his shoulders "but I only did so because I didn't know which you would like. And as for the night gown, the sales consultant was almost as good as you at selling. She convinced me that you would love it! Sorry, it was a moment of weakness. If you would like me to take it all back, I will."

Alicia bit her bottom lip, picked up her cup of coffee and leaned back into her seat. Still a little upset, "I'll make you a deal. If you return all the dresses in the closet, that should cover the cost for one of the dresses in the warehouse."

For a moment there was silence. Jon smiled, "Alright, I'll return the dresses." He placed the cup of coffee on the table and walked to Alicia. He took her cup of coffee out of her hands. "Now, if we are done fighting, I think it's time to make up." Jon leaned towards Alicia and gave her a long slow kiss.

Alicia sighed and tried to resist by placing her hand on Jon's bare chest. She was still fluster with Jon. She didn't want to be known as a leach, but for some reason, her body always had a mind if its own when it came to Jon.

Before she realized what she was doing, she had already stood up and had wrapped her arms around Jon's neck. Jon had found his way up the t-shirt and was squeezing her bare bottom. Alicia squealed with delight. Jon moved his warm strong hands up her silky smooth skin, pressing her body up against his.

"Babe," Jon pulled his lips away from Alicia. With an intense look he announced, "I'm going to take this t-shirt off. Now, you have a choice. I can take it off right here on this table, or I can take it off in the bedroom." He nibbled on her earlobe.

"The bedroom," Alicia murmured. She was still uncomfortable of being completely exposed in front of him. This place, with its very large windows open for the world to look in, made her feel even more awkward.

Jon took her hand and escorted her into the bedroom. He closed the door and with his torso he held her up against the door. He looked straight into her eyes, "Alicia, please believe me when I say that I would never do or say anything to intentionally hurt you. I'm sorry that I offended you with the dresses. That was not my intention."

Alicia looked into his deep hazel eye. It seemed as if she were looking into his soul. She knew he truly meant what he said.

"It just that ..." Jon stopped himself before finishing the sentence. He was about to tell her that all the other women he had dated had always expected to be lavished with expensive gifts, but realized that it might be a mood killer, and right now he wanted her. "I just wanted to surprise you."

"I'm sorry for being so hot headed; I think it's the Latina in me," she smirked. Alicia leaned in for a soft warm kiss. She teased his lips with her tongue.

Within a second, Jon went into primal mode. He slowly trusted his tongue into her mouth and caressed the roof of her mouth. Alicia let out a soft moan. He could feel his excitement rising. Reaching down to the bottom of the white t-shirt he pulled it off the top of her head. Jon took a deep breath at the sight of her. He ran his palms down her shoulder, then down her thighs as he devoured her with his eyes. He shook his head, and took a deep breath, "You are so beautiful."

He honed in on her neck and began to kiss her. Alicia felt a surge of passion. Every inch of her wanted to have Jon. Her body was on fire. Everything down under yearned to be filled. She placed her hands on his shoulders and pulled him in closer. She took her nails and slowly ran them down his perfectly toned back. Jon let out a long moan. When she reached the edge of his boxers, she pulled them off. Jon stepped out of his boxers as they dropped to the floor.

He took Alicia's thighs and pulled her off the floor, her back still to on the door to hold her in place. He thrust his manhood into her. He could feel her fully aroused. He kept her there on the door as he continued to pull in and out.

Alicia couldn't believe that it was possible to feel the way she felt. Her body was internally exploding. Her breathing was erratic, her heart wanted to escape her body, and her womb kept spamming. Having Jon in her made her feel complete. She could feel that she was about to explode into euphoria. She could hear Jon's breathing and knew he was close to coming as well.

Then, suddenly Jon pulled out and put her down on the floor. His heavy breathing made it difficult for him to talk. "I need to get a condom." He turned and walked away towards the night stand. Alicia watched Jon walk away, the image of perfection. His butt muscles flexed as he walked.

Suddenly, Alicia realized she was standing alone by the door she bent down, picked up his t-shirt, and put it on. The moment of elation had passed, and now she just felt empty, and uneasy.

"Jon, it's getting late. I'm going to go clean the kitchen before we leave," she turned opened the door and closed it behind her before Jon could respond.

Jon stood there at the edge of the bed confused. *What the hell just happened?* He followed Alicia into the living room. "Alicia, what's wrong? What happened? Did I say something to upset you? Did I do something wrong?" He stood there completely exposed his hand spread out at his side with a look of confusion on his face.

Alicia smiled and shook her head. *Why is it every time he is near I feel this rush of jubilation? I can't stop wanting him, all of him soul and body.* "I just thought it best if we go to the warehouse and get some work done before we get ready for the Fashion Show. It's already past nine."

As she talked Jon moved closer towards her, by the time she was done rambling, he was standing right in front of her. "I don't believe that's all. Why did you runaway?" He put one hand on her hips, looked at her trembling lips, then into her eyes searching for the truth.

"Are you tired of me already?" He asked as he took his index finger and removed her hair from her eyes.

"No. It's not that." She placed her hand on his bare chest and looked down averting his gaze.

Jon took her chin in his hand and lifted her head so their eye could meet. "Then what it is?"

"I just suddenly felt overwhelmed," she said in a low tone. "It's been five days of complete bliss. You... this place... my new job," she pursed her lips and sighed.

She couldn't bring herself to tell him that she was afraid that it was all going to end soon. That she felt something more than just a fling and that getting any closer would only bring her sadness in the end.

Jon looked into those alluring sweet honey eyes searching for the truth. He could tell that there was more, but he didn't want to push anymore. "Alicia, you are the best thing that has ever happened to me, but I understand if you need your space. If you want me to back off, I will."

The last thing she wanted was to push him away, but at the same time she could not ask him to stay forever. The more time they shared the harder it was becoming to let him go. She tilted her head to the side and looked into his eyes trying to decide what it was she wanted.

She leaned in and gave his a gentle kiss. "Are you for real or are you a dream?"

"I'm real Alicia," he replied as he kissed her with all the passion of a man in love. He felt her temperature rise and her knee weekend. He held her close so she wouldn't fall. They stood there entwined in each other's arms kissing for what seemed an eternity. Jon finally pulled away knowing that he was getting completely aroused by her. "I'm going to go take a shower so we can go. Just leave the kitchen the way it is. I'll clean it when I get back."

He walked off into the bedroom without another word. Alicia finished washing the dishes and placed the pots back in the cover before heading into the bedroom. She needed time to think, cleaning helped, and she also didn't like being told what to do.

Jon was still in the shower when she changed back into her red silk halter dress and sandals. She took her suit, heels and purse, and placed them on the sofa. Soon she heard Jon in the bedroom.

"Jon, can we stop by my place so I can change into a clean suit before we go over the warehouse?" she yelled into the bedroom, unwilling to go in. She sat down on the sofa to wait.

Jon walked into the living room dressed in his clean and pressed suit looking as astonishing as ever. "Sure, are you ready?"

"Yap," she replied as she stood up and picked up her clothes.

******

Jon parked his car behind Alicia's. "Would you like to come in and wait while I change and do my makeup?" she asked as she got out of the car.

Jon joined her. She opened that door and walked in. Jon followed. She put her purse down on the small table by the front door. "Welcome to my home," she radiated with happiness. "It's not much, but it's mine."

"Have a seat where ever you like. I'm just going to put all this in the hamper and change, I'll be right back." She walked into a door that must be the bedroom, but Jon stayed in the puny living room.

The apartment was tiny. There was a small television on a table by the door Alicia had walked into. The sofa was a love seat, that was all that the small room would allow for and a recliner next to it. There was a small eating table behind the sofa and a kitchenette next to the eating area.

The room reminded Jon of his dorm back during his college years. It was quaint, but way too small for what he had gotten accustom to. He sat on a chair at the table. Looking around, Mindy and Alicia had touched up the room with a large wall portrait of the crystal blue waters of Tahiti. The sofa and recliner both had tropical motif pillows and a white shaggy rug on the floor.

"Jon, would you mind if we stopped by the dry cleaners to drop off my suits. I don't have very many and these need to cleaned," Jon heard Alicia's voice through the open door.

He stood and walked over the door. Her room wasn't any bigger than the living room. It had a full size bed and a small dresser with a large mirror. Alicia was looking in the mirror applying her lipstick.

"Not a problem," he replied as he leaned against the door frame of the bedroom door with his hands in his pant pockets. Alicia had changed into a dark blue suit, now she not only looked sexy but deadly professional.

Alicia turned and looked at him. She placed her lipstick back on the dresser. "Okay, I'm ready." She picked up her suits and walked out of her room.

"Nice room." Jon said as she passed him by.

Alicia laughed, "If you like living in a walk-in closet."

Jon frowned, "What do you mean?"

"My room is the size of the walk-in closet at your beach place. I don't mind, its home and I have slept on the street floor so I'm not going to complain," she said as she walked to the front door and grabbed her purse.

Jon simply followed her out the front door.

# Chapter 12: The Warehouse Surprise

After a quick stop at the dry cleaners, they arrived at the down town warehouse. Jon parked in the reserved car port. He walked around and helped Alicia out of the car. As they walked in the front door, they were met by an elderly lady.

"Mr. Whit, so nice to see you. Why didn't you call us, we would have ordered a nice lunch for you. I'm afraid there isn't time of a full course meal. Would you like me to order something from the deli?" said the gray haired motherly lady as she picked up the phone.

Jon walked around the desk and hugged the secretary, "Hi Lily! Yes, deli lunch will be fine. I'll have the usual, and Alicia what would you like, sandwich or salad?"

"A salad will be fine." Alicia replied.

Jon put his arm around Lily's shoulder. "Lily I would like you to meet, Ms. Alicia Garcia. She is the Assistant Manager of the Newport Shop."

He looked at Alicia and said, "This is my very old friend and best secretary in the "From this Day Forward" company, Lily Jones."

"Nice to meet you, Ms. Jones" Alicia smiled and put out her hand.

"Nice to meet you too, Ms. Garcia. Please call me Lily." Lily replied and shook her hand.

Just then Mark walked into the office carrying a clipboard. "Alicia, what are you doing here?"

"I'm here with Mr. Whit." Alicia tried not to blush.

"Lily, Ms. Garcia needs a dress for tonight's Bridal Fashion Show. Could you give her a tour of the warehouse and let her choose whatever she likes for this evening. I'm going to go meet with Parker." Jon walked off into an office.

Lily raised both her brows as Jon walked away, "Well, Ms. Garcia, I guess I should find someone to show you around."

"No need to find someone," Mark responded, "I'll give Alicia the tour."

Alicia felt her stomach turn upside down. *Not only is this a terribly awkward moment, but now I have to put up with Mark for who knows how long?* "Well, I guess I'll be back soon." Alicia told Lily with an uneasy voice.

"No Mark. You're just looking for an excuse to not finish filling out all those order forms. You can stay here in the front office and take the incoming calls while I show Ms. Garcia around." She gave Alicia a warm smile.

Mark frowned and was about to protest, but Lily gave him that look of, *"Don't you dare test me!"* "Alright, I'll stay and answer the phone."

Lily wrapped her arm around Alicia's arm, "Come now Ms. Garcia, let see what we can find for this evening."

"Please call me Alicia," she said with a relived tone.

After a quick tour of the warehouse, Lily and Alicia walked into the showroom. "This is the showroom. Now, let's see if we can find something for you. Did you have anything in mind?" Lily asked in a grandmotherly voice.

"I think I would like something classic and not too flashy. I want to fit in, but not overpower the brides." Alicia responded as she looked around the room.

"I think I have a design you might like. It's a new design scheduled to go out to the shops this summer." Lily walked over to a rack full of evening gowns and pulled out a black floor length a line silk dress.

Lily handed the dress to Alicia. It was a sleeveless round neckline, sheer lace panel to yoke with a fitted waist and silk peplum. Alicia's mouth dropped. "It's perfect."

"Then, try it on," Lily said encouragingly as she walked over to the dressing area.

As Alicia changed into the dress, Lily asked, "So Alicia, have you known Jon long?"

Alicia stepped into the dress and pulled it up. "Not very long, I met him last week at the Anaheim Bride Event Show." She walked out into the showroom to look at herself in the full size mirror.

Lily gave Alicia a huge grin. "It's almost perfect." She walked around Alicia to get a complete 360 degree view. "It will need to be altered to bring up the hem line, but that should only take a few minutes."

Alicia looked at the dress in the mirror. The skirt hugged her hips and the peplum gave her a flirty waist. The sleeveless top showed off her smooth tan skin and the sheer lace panel neckline showed enough cleavage to entice just about anyone.

"It's definitely a Fashion Show dress." Alicia said exuberantly.

"Let me get our in house seamstress. She'll be able to raise the hem so you don't trip." Lily walked over to the phone next to the dressing room. "Hello, Ceci? I need your help in the showroom, I have a dress that needs the hem raised. Yes, we'll wait. Thank you."

Lily turned and looked at Alicia, "Ceci will be here shortly, but while we wait we should probably find the accessories to go with this outfit." Lili walked over to a glass display where the jewelry was kept.

"Oh that's not necessary. I'll be fine without any jewelry." Alicia insisted.

"Alicia you are stunning without jewelry. I know Jon will have a hard time keeping his hands off you, but with this jewelry. I know you will close the deal." She winked at Alicia.

Alicia felt her face change colors. She didn't know what to respond to that statement. "Lily, I'm sure I don't know what you mean by that."

Lily laughed a jolly laugh as she handed Alicia the Princess Kate Inspired bridal chandelier earrings.

"Alicia, I have known Jon since the day he was born. His Mom and Dad first hired me over thirty-five years ago, you know, before he was even born. And in all those years, Jon has never brought a girl to the warehouse or to a Fashion Show. You're the first. So, I know you mean something special to him, even if he hasn't said it to you yet."

Alicia's face turned a brighter red as she took the open teardrop design earrings and put them on. Before she could say another word, she heard the door behind them open.

"Hi, I'm here to hem up a dress." said a bubbly young lady, carrying a basket. Then a gasp, "Alicia, is it really you?"

Alicia turned to see who was speaking. Her heart dropped and so did her jaw. "Cecilia?"

"Si, it's me!" Celi's eyes filled with tears. She stood there stunned.

"Cecila," Alicia ran up and hugged her. The tears ran down her eyes. "Ahi mi cielos! Baby Sis!"

Lily looked perplexed. "You two are related?"

"Yes, Lily this is my baby sister. I haven't seen her in over eight years." Alicia wiped the tears way with her hands. "Ceci there is so much I want to tell you."

Ceci gave Alicia a crooked smile. "Where have you been? Why are you here? Why haven't you call me? Why haven't you called Mom?"

Lily stepped in. "I think you two need some alone time, but this dress needs to be hemmed. Please, focus for a few minutes while you pin it up and start sewing. Then you two can spend the rest of the day talking."

Cecli looked at Lily and then at Alicia, "Please step on the stage so I can pin up the dress."

Alicia didn't want to hem up a dress she wanted to talk, "I think we should talk first."

Ceci snapped, "Dam it Alicia, for once can you do what you're told, instead of trying to get your way!" Ceci eyes pierced through Alicia as she pointed to the stage.

Alicia realized she had no right to insist on anything, not here. This was not her place. She walked onto the stage as she was asked.

Ceci bent down and pinned the hem. "Now please remove the gown so I can get to work."

Alicia stepped off and looked into Ceci's eyes, "Ceclia, I...," she just didn't know how she could apologize for abandoning her sister.

Ceci shook her head, "Please, remove the dress so I can hem it."

Alicia came back out and handed the dress to Ceci. "Here."

"Well, I'm going to go get you your salad and you two can stay in here as long as you need." Lily hugged Alicia and then Ceci before she stepped out of the room.

Ceci sat at the sewing table by the window. Alicia found a chair and pull up close to Ceci. "Ceci, I'm sorry." Alicia whispered.

Ceci started hemming the dress by hand. "What exactly are you sorry for?" she asked without looking up at her.

"For walking out on you, for never calling you, for running away," Alicia replied.

"Why have you never called? Why?" Ceci asked with sorrow in her voice and tears in her eyes.

"At first I couldn't, because I didn't have a phone or money to pay for a phone call. Then as time went by, I just didn't know what to say, so I gave up trying to contact you. I was young and stupid, and for that I'm so sorry." Alicia wanted to hug her, but was afraid of being rejected.

"All this time, Mom and I thought you were dead. We didn't know where you had gone. You broke Mom's heart." Ceci murmured as her hands kept sewing.

"Ceci I know I can never make up for my stupid actions, but I would like to try. Please tell me what can I do to make this better," tears ran down her cheeks.

For a moment there was silence. "You can start by calling Mom, no better yet, you should go and see her." Ceci finally looked up at her.

"Ceci, I don't know if I can face her and dad." Alicia shook her head.

"Dad past away four years ago," Ceci's eyes filled with tears.

Alicia felt a stabbing pain in her chest. Although she couldn't stand the way their father treated them because they were women, he was still her dad.

"Oh Ceci," Alicia hugged her sister and started to cry. "I'm so, so sorry, for everthing! I'll call Mom, I promise."

"You still have to visit her, after you call. Okay?" Ceci patted Alicia's back.

"Okay, I will, I promise." Alicia pulled away and tried to smile. She pulled out her business card from her purse and wrote her cell number on the back. "Here, please call me, we need to get together and catch up."

Ceci took her card and put it the pocket of her smock. "Okay sis, I'll call. Now put this dress on to check if it's right before I press it."

"Alicia, I have your salad." Jon had walked into the showroom. "Lily said you needed some alone time, but I wanted to make sure everything was alright."

He placed the salad on the sewing table and looked into Alicia's eyes. He saw sadness and tears. His nostrils flared and his brow frowned, "Who made you cry?" His primal instinct to protect kicked in.

Alicia quickly walked up to him and wrapped her hands around his waist. "No one Jon, these are happy tears."

Alicia placed her head on his chest. She could feel Jon's body relax, as he wrapped one arm around her waist.

"I would like you to meet Cecilia Garcia, my baby sister." Alicia pulled away and looked at Ceci.

Ceci had been standing there immobile watching as the President of the company had walked into the room. She couldn't believe what was happening. First, she had found her sister and now this gorgeous man was standing before her with his arms around Alicia. She held on to the dress as her only life line to reality.

Jon looked at Ceci and then at Alicia, "I'm sorry, did I hear you correctly? Did you say sister?"

Alicia placed her palm on his chest, nodded and smiled.

"You never mentioned you had a sister." Jon frowned at Alicia and tilted his head, but kept one arm around her waist in protective mode.

"I guess it hadn't come up. I haven't spoken or seen her in, well a long time." Alicia replied with regret.

"Cecilia nice to meet you. I'm Jon Whit." He extended his hand and smiled.

"Ceci shook his hand, "Hello, sir."

"Well I guess Lily was right again." He shook his head and took Alicia's hand. "I'll leave you two to catch up. Alicia I made reservations for dinner at five, will that give you time to get ready?"

"Yes, I'll be ready by then," Alicia nodded.

Without thinking, Jon leaned and kissed her on the temple. "Lily would like to know if she should call our make-up artist and hair stylist to come and help you?"

Alicia blushed realizing that Ceci was present. Alicia shook her head. "I can handle it on my own."

Jon turned towards the door. "I'll be in the main office if you need me," and he walked out.

Ceci handed the dress to Alicia. "Here try it on."

\*\*\*\*\*\*

Ceci returned after a long while carrying the press dress. The dress lay across both Ceci's extended arms. She hung it up on the rack by the fitting room. She turned towards Alicia who was sitting at the sewing table with a compact mirror in one hand and mascara in the other.

"Alicia her is my phone number and the house number. Please call mom as soon as you can." Ceci handed an index card to Alicia.

"Alicia put down the mascara and took the card. "Ceci I would call mom right now, but I just redid my make-up and I don't want to have streaks rolling down my face at the Fashion Show," Alicia held her tears back.

"Esta bien. I don't want you to stain that dress either. It's one of the most expensive dresses we carry." Ceci smiled and pulled up a chair next to Alicia.

Alicia giggled, "Yes, I know."

"So hermana, what's going on between you and Señor Whit? Ceci brows raised as she grinned. "Are you two an item?"

Alicia blushed, "At the moment we are dating."

"But doesn't he live in Michigan?" Ceci asked.

Alicia gave a long sigh, "Yes, he does. We just met last week, so I don't know if it's going to work out between us." She pouted.

Ceci patted her sisters shoulder, "He seems very interested in you, I mean he was really upset when he saw you crying. I thought he would fire me on the spot."

The showroom door opened. "Alicia are you ready? Jon is waiting." Lily had come back.

Alicia quickly stood up. "I was just about to change into the dress." She ran into the fitting room with the dress in hand.

Lily and Ceci waited for Alicia to come out. Both Lily and Cei beamed with delight as they watched Alicia sashay into the showroom with the pressed black lace dress and those sparkling earrings.

"Alicia you look beautiful," Ceci gasped and hugged her.

Lily took Alicia by the hand. "You look good enough to be one of the models in on the run way. Now, come on." Lily placed her arm around Alicia's arm.

*****

Jon's jaw dropped at the sight of Alicia. Her smoky eyes were alluring. Her nude lips enticing. Those sparkling earrings tempted him to nibble. That black tight lace that stretched against her torso showing off just the right amount of bust was arousing. The peplum skirt teased him to squeeze her bottom and those tan bare arms called to be caressed. "You, look," he shook his head, "you look…" He couldn't find the words to describe her. Finally he said, "Captivating!"

Alicia smiled, "Shall we go?" She whispered trying to break the spell.

"Yes, let's," Jon placed his palm on his stomach and held his elbow out so Alicia could wrap her hand around.

"Wait one moment." Lily screeched. "You can't go without a wrap." She placed a creamy white cashmere body wrap across her shoulders. "Not that I think Jon will let you freeze, but every lady needs a shawl." She winked at Alicia.

# Chapter 13: The Fashion Show

After dinner Jon and Alicia arrived for the Fashion Show at the Beverly Hotel. The banquet room was full of seated businessmen and women in the Bridal Industry, all waiting for the show to begin.

The lights dimmed. Jon handed Alicia a notepad and a pen. "Here just in case you see something you like. Make a note of it so you can refer back to it after the show."

Alicia simply nodded.

The announcer came on stage and was flooded with a spot light. "Welcome to the Summer Line Fashion Show. Tonight we have the pleasure of introducing some of the new up and coming designer in the wedding industry. We hope you enjoy the show."

The music started and the bevy of models dressed in white began to appear. Alicia was quickly captivated by the ambiance. The dresses where outstanding and the way the models glides across the runway was hypnotic.

Then a tall blond floated across the floor. It was Janet. Jon's body tensed up, but he did not say a word. Alicia however did notice the change in Jon's demeanor. Soon after, Cindy and Katrina paraded down past them as well. The bright spot lights however made it difficult for the models to look out into the audience.

Alicia took note of two designers she thought might be worth perusing. When the show was over the lights came back on and everyone stood up to mingle. Jon turned to Alicia, "Did you see any designs that you thought we should consider."

"Yes, I did. I thought that Sue Kim's line would be perfect. She has a fresh new bohemian look that we currently do not offer, and Mr. Collin's designs have a very classic look." Alicia looked at Jon to see if he agreed with her choices.

"Why Ms. Garcia, I never would have guessed you would be this good and choosing designers. I must admit, I'm impressed. I would have to agree with you about both artists." Jon smiled. "Why don't I get us some drinks before we approach the designers?"

Alicia nodded and watched Jon walk away into the crowd around the bar. She stood there holding her clutch purse in one hand and the shawl around her arm. She noticed Mr. Collin's was speaking with another gentleman only a few feet way. Each was holding a drink in their hand. She thought it would be the perfect moment to approach.

"Mr. Collin, it's so nice to meet you. I must congratulate you on your presentation this evening. I love your work." Alicia gave him a big smile and extended her hand.

"Why thank you." He placed one hand over his heart and with the other he shook Alicia's hand. "I'm glad you enjoyed my newest designs, but please call me Timothy."

The gentleman standing to Timothy's right wore a very expensive black suit. He was tall but not as tall as Jon. He wasn't bad looking, but he was not drop dead gorgeous either. He seemed very impressed by Alicia, and couldn't stop staring at her. "Which dress did you like the best from Mr. Collin's line?"

Alicia knew showing her hand to a competitor was not a wise thing to do. "I thought the elegant strapless lace sheath was amazing. I loved the way the lace draped at the bottom," she replied as she opened her purse. Most of it was true. This dress was one of the top three she had liked but not the one she loved.

"Timothy. We at 'From this Day Forward,' would love to discuss your design with you." She handed him a business card, batted her eyelashes and showed off her smile. "Mr. Whit will probably ask to set up an appointment for us to meet, but here is my card. If you have any questions, please feel free to call me."

Timothy took the card and read it. "Yes, Ms. Garcia. I will definitely wait to hear from you."

"Please call me Alicia." She grinned.

"Okay. Oh, I'm sorry but I see a dear old friend over by the bar. If you'll excuse me," Timothy waved and walked away.

"So Ms. Garcia, you work for Jon Whit? He is very lucky to have you as his design consultant. I don't think I have ever seen Jon bring a consultant to a show before." The man in the dark suit was fixated on Alicia. "I'm sorry. I haven't properly introduced myself. I'm Max James. The CEO of 'The Knot.'" He held out his hand.

"Nice to meet you, Mr. James, but I'm not Mr. Whit's design consultant." Alicia shook his hand trying to be polite. "I'm the Assistant Manager at the Newport Beach Shop. Mr. Whit simply thought it might be nice to get a woman's perspective."

Max reluctantly released Alicia's hand. "You mean, you are not in his design department. Oh, I think that is a terrible mistake on Jon's part. If you ever decide to move up to the design department and earn some real money. Please give me a call." Max reached into his pocket and handed Alicia a business card.

Alicia took his card and placed it in her purse. "Thank you Mr. James, but I am currently very happy as the Assistant Manager."

"The invitation to join our team is an open invitation. You are welcome to join us anytime, be it next week or in ten years. We are always looking for smart bright and lovely people to join our Knot Family.

Alicia blushed. "Thank you for the job offer."

Jon walked up to Alicia. "So, Max how have you been?" He handed a wine glass to Alicia.

"Thank you," she said and she took the glass from Jon.

"I have been well, sales are going well. I haven't seen you at one of these shows in a while. Where have you been?" Max asked as he took a drink from his iced glass.

"I've been attending the Show in New York. It's been a while since I've been out here in California." Jon replied.

Alicia perused the crowd looking for Sue Kim, but could not find her in the mass of people. She did however see the buffet table. A platter of honey covered cheese caught her eye. She had never tasted honey and cheese before and thought this would probably be the only time she would get to taste it. "Please excuse me, I'll be over by the buffet table, if you need me."

Alicia walked away without glancing back, but she could feel two pair of eyes on her. She picked up a plate before walking up to the cheese platter. She was about to put down the wine glass to pick up a slice of cheese when she heard her.

"So Alicia what are you doing here?" Janet asked in a cold voice.

Alicia turned to face the tall blonde. "I'm here with Mr. Whit looking for next season's designs." She clutched her wine glass.

Janet looked directly at Alicia, "Oh Alicia, please tell me you are not that naïve." She took a sip of her wine glass. "Jon isn't really interested in you. He's just using you, sooner or later he's going to discard you like he does all the women in his life. Jon loves his job more than anything else in life. Jon has slept with half the models in this show. Every girl here knows that Jon is good to play around with, but don't expect him to be a serious contender. Besides you're not really his type." She looked at Alicia from head to toe and walked away.

*What a bitch! If I weren't at the Show I would punch her across the face.* Alicia could feel her body shaking in anger. She just stood there trying to calm herself. She turned to look for Jon, but he had found Sue Kim and was in an energetic conversation. She couldn't bother him at the moment. She decided to stick around the buffet table, even though she was no longer hungry.

All of the sudden Alicia was blinded by a bright flash, then another flash, and a third flash. When she was able to see again, she realized that a photographer was walking around her taking photos of guests.

"Are you okay?" a jolly older gentleman asks.

"Yes, I was just startled," Alicia replies as she blinks trying to get her sight back.

"I know you are not one of the models because I saw you in the audience, but you certainly could have fooled me." The chubby man said. "Could I get you a drink?"

"Thank you, but I already have a drink." Alicia said politely. "If you'll excuse me, I have to find Mr. Whit." She walked away before the stranger could ask her any more questions.

Again a flash of light hit her in face, "Please, could you stop blinding me with your camera." She put her hand out to avoid being blinded.

"Alicia," Jon walked up to her. "What's going on?" he asked.

"Mr. Whit could you please pose with your date, we would love to include a picture in the up-coming summer issue of Wedding Dress Magazine," the photographer bellowed. "Is that one of your evening wear dresses?"

Jon tried to polity decline, "Yes, it is one of the new designs for the coming summer, but I think you have taken enough pictures of Ms. Garcia."

Alicia wrapped her arm around Jon's arm. "I guess one more photo won't hurt, plus it will help promote the new design." She smiled a weary smile.

They stood for a few minutes while the photographer took more photos. "Thank you so much. I'll send the proofs to your office when they are ready."

More people had started to stare and whisper. Too many eyes made Alicia uneasy, and the jolly old man kept winking at her. She took her shawl and wrapped it around her torso. "Jon, it's getting late, can we leave now? I need to be at work early tomorrow."

Jon took the wine glass from Alicia's hand, and placed it on a small table. "Sure we can go, but you don't have to go to work tomorrow until after two. I emailed Mindy earlier today letting her know that you would be at the Fashion Show this evening. So she won't be expecting you until late in the afternoon." Jon smiled.

Alicia became irritated. She hated when decision were made for her. *This is why I left home! I don't need a man to tell me what I can and can't do!* "Please Jon dive me home."

Jon was confused. "Alicia, are you upset?"

"No, just tired. Too much has happened today. I'm sorry. I have really enjoyed this evening." She slipped her hand around Jon's arm, glanced around and saw that the crowd was still staring. "Please, let's go."

Jon saw Janet glaring at Alicia with a smirk on her face as they walked towards the exit. "Did Janet say something to you?"

"Yes, she did," Alicia kept walking but did not meet Jon's eyes.

"What did she say?" Jon asked in a demanding tone.

"She said that I'm not your type, and by the stares from the crowd. It seems that others feel the same," she said in a hazy voice.

Jon froze at the door, "Well if they are going to talk, we should give them something to talk about." He turned towards Alicia took her chin in his hand and placed a sweet kiss on her lips. "I've been dying to kiss you all night, and I know most of the men in this room are wishing they were me right now."

Alicia's irritation with the jolly old man, the pushy photographer, the bitch of Janet, and Jon's assumption that he could make choices on her behalf evaporated. Now she just saw Jon, the man who owned her heart and soul, no one else mattered. She didn't know what to say. She felt a surge of warmth fall over her.

Jon took her hand and wrapped his fingers around hers. "Shall we go?" They walked out into the hotel holding hands.

Jon asked, "Would you like to spend the night here in the suite, or would you rather go back to the beach?"

Just the thought of spending the night in the same building Janet and her vulture friends were still mingling made her want to hurl. "I would prefer going home." Alicia sighed.

# Chapter 14: The Key to Her Heart

The car pulled up behind Alicia's car. "Here we are," Jon said with both hand on the wheel. "Before you go, I just wanted to let you know that I have been trying very hard to keep my hands off you since we left the warehouse."

He reached over, took Alicia's hand, and kissed it. He reached into his pocket, took out a key, and placed it in her hand. "I want you to have the extra key to the beach home. I know it's not your home, but I'd like it if you thought of it as your place."

Alicia didn't know what to say. She looked at the key. *Does he want me to move in? I like my place! Plus, he's not sticking around for very long.* She shook her head. "Jon, I don't understand. You're giving me a key to a townhome that isn't your home. It's just a space that you are currently staying in. How long are you planning on staying here?"

Jon looked at Alicia. "I want to stay as long as I can. The townhome has a six month lease on it. So, technically I can stay here for six months, longer if I renew the lease. I will probably have to travel every few weeks, but I can always come back and work from here. My family has already voiced their dislike of me renting a place here, but I think I can make it work." He paused for a moment and ran his thumb down Alicia's cheek. "I don't understand what has happened, but your presence makes me feel alive and happy. I don't want to be alone anymore. I want to be a part of your life, if you'll let me."

Alicia's eyes filled with tears but she fought them back. She bit her lower lip to stop from crying. *He wants to stay here for me.* She couldn't believe that this very handsome, rich and well educated man wanted her in his life. "Jon, are you sure you want to stay here? I'm sure your parents won't disapprove of you see a girl like me."

"What are you talking about?" Jon frowned.

"Seriously Jon, I have no formal education. I'm Mexican. I can barely make ends meet. I don't exactly fit your tall blond and blue eyed girlfriend type." Those last words hurt saying, but Janet's comments kept ringing in her ears.

"Alicia, you are more beautiful than any model I have ever dated. You have a true beauty that radiates from within. You think that everyone was staring at you tonight because you didn't fit in, but you are wrong. They were all staring because they could not believe how genuinely beautiful you are. You're smart, charming, charismatic, seductive and honest. Those are qualities that most of the people in the hall have never possesses. The women where jealous of the way you captivated the men, and the men just wanted to undress you." Jon eyes yearned to kiss her.

With every word Alicia's body filled with desire. She couldn't understand why Jon wanted her, but she knew that she wanted him just as badly. Not because he was rich or handsome, but because he believed that she was special.

Alicia took the key and put it in her purse. She ran her fingers through her hair. Then she took his hand, "My bed in not has large or as comfortable as your beach bed, and I do have a roommate just across the hall, but I would really like if you spent the night."

Jon eye's glistened and he smiled from ear to ear. Without a second to lose he jumped out of the driver's seat and came around to open the passenger's door. Alicia took his hand and stepped out the car.

They walked up to the front door. Alicia unlocked it and stepped inside. Jon stood in the doorway. He whispered, "You do understand that if I come in, Mindy is going to find out about us? There won't be any doubt that you and I, are a couple."

Alicia nodded. "I understand, but right now I just want you more than anything else." She took his tie in her hand and pulled him into the tiny apartment.

Jon quietly closed the door behind him. "I guess we should try not to wake Mindy."

Alicia took his hand and let him into her room. "I'll try not to moan too loudly." Once in her room, she closed the door and locked it, just in case Mindy decided to visit her in the morning.

# Chapter 15: Getting Fired

The last six months had been perfect. Alicia couldn't be happier. Jon had stayed for a week more before leaving for a business trip. They had spent every day together before he left. While he was on his trips they had spoken every night. Sometimes they would text during the day or send each other email. Alicia missed having him around, but enjoyed talking to him over the phone in the evenings.

Jon would go off for a week and come up to work from his beach home for a few days out of the month. When Jon was in town, Alicia practically lived over at his place, but when he was gone, she would go home, and visit her sister and mom.

Today however, Alicia sat at her desk infuriated. She couldn't believe Katrina could be such a birde-zilla. She knew that Janet had something to do with Katrina's behavior today, but there was nothing see could do.

Two days earlier Katina had asked that Alicia personally assist in the dress alterations. After coming in for a fitting, Katrina had decided she wanted some changes made to the dress. Alicia and Connie, their seamstress, had advised her that the changes to the dress would alter the look and would be impossible to redo the original design once the cuts were made. Katrina had insisted that she wanted her dress to be special and unique. So Alicia had approved the changes.

Today Katrina had come in for a final fitting, and was unhappy with the alteration. She accused Alicia and Connie of butchery. She didn't like the way the dress draped. Katrina had stormed out of the dressing area yelling that Alicia was a terrible shop manager, and that she should not be trusted. She stood in the middle of the shop and demanded a full refund on the $10,000 dress. "Now I'm going to have to go out and find a new dress and the wedding is so close, that I don't know if I'll find anything! So give me back my money!" she had ordered.

Alicia couldn't refund her money, without the shop owner's approval. Alicia had requested the alternations and had understood that the changes would not be reversible. Also, the shop did not have $10,000 on hand to simply write her a check.

Alicia had agreed, to get back to her within 24 hours. Letting her know what could be done about the refund. Katrina had stormed out and threatened that this was not over.

"Hey, I just heard about what happened this morning. Are you okay?" Mindy asked as she sat down in front of Alicia's desks.

"Yea, I'm fine, but now I have to call corporate to find out about the refund," Alicia sighed.

"I can call them if you'd like." Mindy offered.

"No, that's okay. I'll do it. This is my mess, and I have to clean it up." Alicia frowned as she played with a pen in her hands.

Mindy stood up, "Okay sweetie, I'll be out on the floor if you need me."

"Thanks. I'll be out as soon as I finish my call," Alicia looked up at Mindy and tried to give her a smile.

Alicia picked up the phone. "Hello, this Alicia Garcia from the Newport Beach shop in California, may I speak to whomever is in charge of refunds."

"Hi Alicia, this is Grace, I'm Mr. Whit's secretary. He's usually the one who contacts the shop owner and deals with irritate brides, but he is currently out of the country. So, I'll let Mr. Steven Whit know. He'll contact you by tomorrow morning. Will that be alright?" said the voice over the phone.

Alicia kept spinning the pen in her hand, "Yes that will be fine thank you Grace." She hung up the phone. *I guess I can send Jon an email letting him know what happened.* Alicia didn't like calling him during the day and bothering him so she turned towards the computer to write and email.

******

"Hi bro! What going on? Jon asked as he sat in café drinking some tea.

"I have a problem and need your input." Steven replied over the phone.

"Okay, shoot." Jon looked out of the café window.

"I got a call early this morning from Katrina Jackson. She was very upset over the alterations to her wedding gown. She claims that Alicia approved the changes knowing that it would ruin the dress. I tried to calm her down, but she just insisted that I give her a refund. She has already gone on the internet and put up bad reviews on all the Social Media sites. She claims that the management at the Newport Beach shop is incompetent and has bad customer service."

Jon opened his lap top. "What do you plan to do about Katrina?"

"I was planning on offering her a replacement dress, to appease her, but I don't think that's going to be enough to stop the barrage of bad publicity we're going to get on the internet," said the voice on the phone

"What else were you thinking?" Jon asked as he scanned his screen.

"I think Katrina is out to ruin Alicia, and we need to do something to protect the shop and Alicia."

Jon nodded, "Yes, I think you are right. I know Janet is behind this mess, but I can't prove it. What if you fire Alicia? That will protect the store and save Alicia's reputation."

There was silence on the other end of the phone. "You think I should fire Alicia?"

"No not exactly. I want you to tell Katrina that the management at Newport Beach will be revamped. Then, I would like you to give Alicia a month vacation with pay. Let her know that she will not be returning to the Newport Beach shop as an Assistant Manager, but that you will get back to her as to where her new position will be. That will give me a chance to give Alicia her own store." He paused, then went on, "I know she won't accept me helping her outright, she's too self reliant, but if she has no choice, I can offer her a shop that she can run."

"Jon are you sure you want me to do that? She might not forgive you for asking me to demote her? I can move her to another one of my shops as a Manager. I think that would make her feel better."

"Steven, I don't want her as a Manager, I want to make she the store owner. She deserves to have her own store," Jon kept scrolling down his screen.

"You want to hand her a store? Do you know what you are saying? There is no way Mom and Dad are going to like that you are giving away Franchises."

For a moment Jon stayed silent trying to decide if he could finally say what he had wanted to say for some time now. "Steve, I'm in love with her and I want her to be happy. I know she wants to be independent and dreams of someday having her own store. I want to provide her the opportunity."

Now it was Steve who was silent. "Did you just use the L word? Have you told her?"

"No, I haven't told her, but I plan to as soon as I get back. It's getting harder for me to travel. I don't want to leave her behind anymore. I want to bring her with me, but I can't if she's managing a store." Jon use his right hand to type while holding the phone up with his left.

"Okay broe, I'll demote her, but I hope you know what you are doing. If Alicia is as proud as you say, she's going very upset about this."

"I'll fix it, Stevie," he said as he smiled.
******

Alicia knew that Jon was in Toronto Canada for the entire week, but she had hoped he would call her that evening. She sat on her bed and opened her lap top hoping to see a response to her email, but there was no response. *Maybe the time difference is making it hard for him to call me. I'll check in the morning.*

Mindy popped her head in, "So, did you hear back from Jon yet?" She walked in and sat on Alicia's bed.

"No not yet. It might be the time change that's causing us to miss each others calls."Alicia closed the lap top and put it on her nightstand.

"Maybe." Mindy responded as she rubbed Alicia's knee. "I'm sure he's probably busy."

"Yea, I think you might be right. I'll check in again in the morning. What do you think is going to happen with Katrina?" Alicia rubbed her tired eyes.

"The owner will probably give her a refund, and write the dress off as damaged or try to sell it as an irregular closeout item." Mindy shrugged. "I'm sure everything will be fine."

"I don't know, it's a huge amount of money," I don't think the shop owner is going to be happy to give a $10,000 refund." Alicia lay back on her bed. "I just want this day to be over. Good night." She rolled over and closed her eyes.

Mindy sighed, "Good night bestie, what time are you scheduled to go into work tomorrow?"

"I have to be there at ten." Alicia responded but didn't open her eyes. Mindy got up and walked back to her room.
******

Alicia's cell phone began to ring around eight in the morning. She ran out of the bathroom and back into her room. The phone was on the night stand next to her laptop. She picked it up hoping it was Jon, but the number was unknown. She answered, "Hello?"

"Alicia?" said the voice on the other end, this is Mr. Whit."

The voice sounded like Jon's. "Jon is that you?" Alicia asked unsure of who was on the other end of the phone.

"Um, no it's Steven Whit."

Alicia stood there motionless. She had stopped breathing and could not find her voice.

"Hello, is anyone there?" Steven asked.

"Yes, it's Alicia, Mr. Whit," she struggled to get the words out.

"I'm returning your phone call. Grace did tell you that I would be calling didn't she?"

"Yes, yes she did, I just didn't expect a personal call." Alicia admitted still unable to move.

"Ms. Garcia the reason I'm calling you on your personal phone is because Katrina has been on a rampage to discredit you and the Newport Beach shop. So I need to take immediate action, if we are to save your shop's credibility. Do you understand?"

"Yes Mr. Whit, I understand. The store should not suffer for mistakes made by me." Alicia whispered.

"I think it's best if you take as few weeks of vacation starting immediately. That way Katrina thinks she has won. I'll have Grace contact you later today, to let you know which other shop you will be working at." Silence. "Ms. Garcia, I don't think we will be able to find you an Assistant Manager Position right away, so you will have your choice of a few shops in the area that have consultant positions."

"I understand, Mr. Whit." I'll await Grace's call." Alicia was shaking.

"Alicia, this was not an easy decision, I spoke to Jon before I made my final decision. He agreed that removing you from Katrina's direct line of fire was the best choice. Please understand."

"Thank you, for your call Mr. Whit." Alicia hung up the phone. She felt like the wind had been knot out of her. She sat that the edge of the bed trying to gasp for air. Tears ran down her face. *I can't believe I've been let go. I can't go back to being a consultant. I won't go back! So, Jon will take his brother's call, but won't respond to my emails!*

Alicia called Mindy, "Mindy, I've been fired! I have been asked not to come into work anymore. I'm sorry, but you'll have to close today."

"Alicia I don't believe it! Why??

"Mr. Steven Whit said it was to protect the shop from any more bad publicity." Alicia whimpered.

"Oh sweetie, what are you going to do? Have you spoken to Jon?"

"No, I haven't been able to reach Jon. So today I'm going to sulk and tomorrow I'll figure something out. You know me. I can't be stop and won't be stopped. I'll land on my feet. I'll see you later."

Alicia sank into your bed. She tucked a pillow under her chin and hugged it. Thick tears ran down her face. *I won't be stopped. I'm not going back. The day I walked out of my dad's home I never went back. My will power is stronger that any man. I'm unstoppable! I will not go back to being a consultant, I've worked too hard to move up in this company!* She hoped that she could believe every word her brain was thinking, but her heart was acing.

*Why has Jon not called me back? Why did Jon do this to me? Why did he have his brother fire me? Is he tired of me? Does he want to get rid of me?* The longer Alicia wallowed the more doubt overtook her thoughts and soul.

She fell asleep crying, feeling sorry for herself, and defeated. She awoke when she heard Mindy arrive in the evening.

Mindy popped her head into Alicia's room. "Hey, how are you doing?" She walked in with a quart of chocolate ice cream, two bowls and two spoons.

"I got you some ice cream. It's your favorite, dark chocolate." She handed a spoon to Alicia as she sat on the bed next to her. "Have you been in bed all day?"

Alicia sat up, took the spoon and the container. She scooped up a large spoon of ice cream and put it in her bowl. She nodded. "Yea, I've been lying here all day."

"I still don't know what to tell you. Have you heard from Jon yet?"

"No, I think he's just avoiding me now. I sent him another email and a text message, but he hasn't responded. I did get an email from corporate. They are offering me a choice of consultant positions in Santa Ana, Westminster, or Seal Beach. I have two weeks to decide, and then I have two more weeks to prepare for my new position." Alicia took another spoonful of ice cream.

"What have you decided?" Mindy whispered as she scooped up a spoonful of ice cream.

Alicia shrugged her shoulders and shook her head, "Today is a pity party day not a day for choices. Tomorrow I'll figure something out."

Mindy and Alicia sat on her bed eating ice cream. They didn't talk any more just ate in silence. Mindy left Alicia alone to finish the ice cream. She needed to get up early the next day to go to work.

# Chapter 16: The Plan

It was almost noon, when Alicia finally rolled out of bed. She took a shower hoping it would wash away the heartache, but it hadn't. Today was a new day and she was determined to make some hard choices. She had left her sales position at the phone company to better her life. Now, she had no choice, but to find somewhere else that would allow her to grow. Last night had been a long night. She had spent it mostly thinking. She was brushing her hair when her cell phone rang.

"Alicia, how are you doing?" Jon asked.

"I've been trying to contact you for two days. Why hadn't you called me back?" Alicia felt her blood boil. She was angry that Jon had not been there when she needed his support. She was angry that he had agreed to have her fired. She was angry that Janet had caused her to doubt Jon.

"I've been at meetings all day and night. We are in the middle of negotiations to open up some shops here in Toronto?" Jon tried to explain.

There was silence. "Alicia why aren't you saying anything?"

"And what exactly would you like me to say. Maybe you would like me to thank you for having your blood sucking ex fire me." Alicia snapped.

"Steven fired you? He said he was going to find a new store for you."

"He offered me a demotion and four weeks to recover from the blow." She hissed.

"You sound mad. Why?"

Alicia's eye almost popped out of her head. Her voice raised, "Are you serious! You think that I should be happy that I was demoted? Should I be grateful that your brother didn't just out right fire me? I did nothing wrong, and I'm the one who has to pay for that vindictive bitch!"

"Alicia, I can understand that you think a change in venue is a bad thing, but I agreed to it to protect you from any more defamatory statements."

Alicia was seething. "Thank you for your help Jon. Now I have some choices I need to consider. So if you'll excuse me I have to go." She hung up the phone. *He did it to protect me? Bull! He did it to protect his company from bad publicity.*

Alicia walked over to her dresser drawer and pulled out her clutch purse, the one she had taken to the Fashion Show with Jon. She found the card and read it, "Mr. Max James, CEO of 'The Knot.'"

The phone rang. She pick it up. It was Jon again. Alicia let it go to voice mail, then she dialed. "Hello, Mr. James. This is Alicia Garcia, we met at the Fashion Show back in March."

"Oh, yes, Alicia the woman with an eye for design but not a design consultant. It's nice to hear from you. Have you decided to join 'The Knot' family?"

Alicia could hear Max smiling. "Mr. James, I'm calling to see if there are any positions available in your organization. I would love to apply if there is."

"Alicia I told you that you are always welcomed here. You don't need to apply."

"Mr. James, I'm very grateful for your offer, but I would rather apply and be interviewed just like everyone else. I would like an opportunity to make sure that my joining your family would be beneficial for both of us."

"Very well. Would you be able to attend a job interview tomorrow at 11:00 am?"

"Will the interview be held at your corporate office, in Altadena?" Alicia asked with trepidation.

"Yes, just come into the office, and tell Holly you are here to see me for the Designer Position."

"Thank you, Mr. James. I'll be there." Alicia hung up the cell and walked into the living room.

Her appetite had returned, she realized that she had not had solid food in over 24 hours, so she decided to have some scrambled eggs and bacon.

As she sat down to eat her breakfast, the phone rang. It was a text message from Jon. "Alicia we need to talk, I'll be back in two days. Please, call me back."

Her resentment towards Jon made her breakfast feel like she had just swallowed stones, it pained her. At this moment she wanted nothing to do with Jon Whit. She was mostly angry with herself. She knew when she met him that dating him was a mistake, a mistake that would cause her pain and the loss of her job. It was time to give up the fantasy. Jon didn't want her it was all just a game to him. *If he really cared would he have allow his brother to demote me?*

She finish cleaning up the kitchen and decided to stop by Jon's beach home one last time. There were a few items she needed to retrieve before she left.

******

Alicia drove up to her mother's house in her new car after picking up her clothes from Jon's place. She knew that no matter where she went, she would still have to send Jon a check every month. Although the car was in her name, Jon had paid for it when her junk car finally died. She promised to pay him back for the car, and she planned on keeping her promise.

Alicia knocked on the door. A round older lady with a full head of gray answered the door. "Alicia, que haces aqui? What are you doing here?" Her mother questioned as she hugged her.

"I came to spend the day. I have a job interview tomorrow, so I decided to spend my day here with you." Alicia said as she stepped in.

"But I thought you already had a job. Que paso?" she asked with concern.

"A was demoted, and given a choice of stores. I liked my job and I liked working with Mindy, so I think I'm just going to see if I can find something else that I like." Alicia said as she sat down on the living room sofa.

"Well, you have always been very stubborn, so there is not point for me to convince you to take the demotion." Her mom walked into the kitchen. "Would you like some tea?"

Alicia knew it was a rhetorical question, her mom was bring tea weather she wanted it or not.

"So where is this interview?" her mom came back in the room and handed her the cup of tea.

"It's in Altadena. Still here is Southern California. It's a position as a design consultant." Alicia took a sip. Her cell phone rang. It was Jon again. She clenched her jaw and frowned.

"Quien es?" her mother asked.

"It's Jon." Alicia shoved the phone in her purse after turning it off.

"Isn't that your boyfriend?"

"Yes, he was my boyfriend, but I don't want to see him or speak to him at the moment." Alicia sighed. "Mom, can I spend the night here? I know Jon will come looking for me, but I don't want to talk to him until after my interview. I don't want the distraction. I need to make a good impression, and Jon always makes me lose focus."

Her mother smiled at her, "That sounds like love, mija. When a man makes you unable to focus and makes it difficult to be rational, it usually means you're in love." She placed her hand on Alicia's. "Does he love you, too?"

"I don't know mom. He has never said it. So, I don't know." Alicia could feel the tears in her eyes, but she fought them back. *Yesterday was pity day, today is moving forward day!*

Her mother could tell that Alicia was struggling, "Of course you can stay as long as you want. You have been gone for so long, that I wish you would stay forever. But first you must help me prepare for dinner. I need you to help me clean the beans."

Alicia's face lit up with joy, "Are we having bean burritos for dinner?" She jumped out of the sofa. "Finally, some real Mexican food!"

Alicia's mom laughed, "Vamos, let's get to work."

****** 

Ceci, Phelipe, and the twins arrived for dinner. "This is a surprise," Ceci said as she hugged Alicia. "Where is Jon?" She looked around the living room.

"She's here by herself," their mother said. "Now leave it alone."

Ceci looked at Alicia with an inquisitive look, "Que paso?"

Alicia didn't want to talk about it, "I'll tell you later. Right now I'm hungry."

Everyone sat around the kitchen table and had dinner. Alicia loved the way homemade beans tasted. She had missed them more that she realized. It was wonderful to be surrounded by family. Alicia felt a warm feeling in her heart. *I can't believe I left them, but I'm glad they took me back.*

After dinner, Alicia and Ceci stayed in the kitchen to clean up. Phelipe, the twins and their mother had gone out to the backyard for a round of soccer. Grandma was the cheering section.

"Okay, Alicia. It's time to spill the beans. What the heck happen with Jon? Did you do something to screw things up? Or did he?" Ceci was always so direct, it reminded Alicia of herself.

Alicia told her the whole story. She started when she met Janet, and ended with how Steven Whit had demoted her.

"So why are you running away from Jon? He didn't fire you, his brother did." Ceci dried a dish.

"Ceci, he agreed with his brother that it was the best thing to do. He said he did it to protect me from anymore attackes, but I don't believe that. I think he did to save the shop, not me." The little voice in her head kept repeating Janet's words. *He loves his job more than anything else in the world.* She dried a plate and stacked it on top the of Ceci's pile.

"The thought that Jon has only been toying with me hurts too much to continue seeing him. Mom thinks I'm in love, but right now I just want to cry." Alicia tried to hold back the tears.

Ceci put down the plate and hugged Alicia. "I'm sorry, that you got demoted, and I'm sorry you're confused about Jon's feeling towards you, but I'm afraid mom is right. You are in love that's why it hurts so much. But, you should at least let him explain himself in person."

"Tomorrow I have an interview for a new position with another wedding company. So, I don't want or need the distraction. After the interview, I'll think about seeing Jon." Alicia swiped her hair away from her eyes. "For now let me enjoy being home again." She smiled.

*******

Jon would have preferred to spend another day negotiating, but knowing that Alicia was angry and wouldn't return his call made his unable to continue. He accepted their terms and left. He took the next flight out of Toronto.

When he arrived in Newport Beach, he went by Alicia's place but her car was not there. He still got out and knocked but there was no answer. He called her on the phone and pleaded for her to pick up, but there was no answer.

He stopped by the shop, but Mindy had not seen Alicia since early that morning, and she had only confide in her, that she needed to think about her options. Jon drove to his beach home, hoping he would find her sitting on the terrace watching the waves, but when he arrived, he didn't see her car. He walked in and found Alicia's key on the kitchen table, the key that he had given to her. Jon ran into the bedroom and opened all the drawers, she had taken all her personal belongs, but had left behind every item Jon had given her. Jon sat on the bed, with a sense of emptiness and sorrow. *Why Alicia, why?*

Jon called her a few more times that evening. He had texted her, and emailed her, but no answer. Finally the jet lag set in, and Jon fell asleep in his bed alone for the first time since he had moved in. *Where are you, Alicia?*

The next day, Jon had a plan. He drove to the warehouse to talk to Ceci. If anyone would know where Alicia had gone, it was her sister. Since they had found each other, they would text each other almost every other day. So, Jon was sure Ceci would know her where about.

"Good morning Ceci." Jon said as he walked into the sewing room.

Ceci was in the middle of altering a dress for one of the photo shoots. She was startled when she heard a man's voice. "Oh, good morning Mr. Whit, I'm sorry I jumped it's just that I wasn't expecting anyone."

"No, I'm the one who should apologize, I shouldn't have come in so abruptly. Ceci, the reason I'm here is because I'm looking for Alicia. Have you heard from her." Jon sat on a chair next to Ceci.

"Yes, I have heard from her," Cecil tried not to look Jon directly in the eyes.

"Where is she? I've been calling, texting, and emailing for hours, but she won't answer. I've driven by her place, but she hasn't been home since yesterday morning. Mindy doesn't know where she is, and I'm starting to worry that something has happened to her."

Ceci looked up to meet Jon's eyes, "Mr. Whit, Alicia is upset, but she is fine. I can't tell you where she is, because I don't know. She wouldn't tell me. She knew you might try to get me to tell you."

Jon looked at Ceci with sadness in his eye, "I never meant to upset her. I would nerve intentionally want to cause her any harm. Ceci I agreed to the demotion to protect her from Katrina, it was only going to be temporary until I found her something better. I tried to tell her, but she hung up on me, and now she won't return my calls." Jon slouched and ran both hands through his hair. "Why, does she always run away?"

Ceci sighed, "Mr. Whit, Alicia is defiant, headstrong and proud. She will do what she believes is best for herself. She left home eight years ago, because father was too controlling. He tried to tell her how to live her life thinking he was doing it for her own good, but Alicia chose to live on the street rather than losing her integrity. She is self reliant and will not play by anyone's rules but her own. If she wants to speak to you, she will contact you. If she's not ready to accept what she had done is wrong, then you might not hear from her for a long time."

Jon sat there and stared at Ceci, "I won't accept that. I'm going to find her, no matter how long it takes. I have to tell her why I did what I did, and then if she wishes that I leave her alone, I will. But, I will not abandon her, without hearing that she doesn't want me in her life anymore." He stopped talking remembering that it was Ceci's father who had allowed Alicia to live on the streets without going to find her.

# Chapter 17: A New Day

After spending the night in her childhood bedroom, Alicia was ready to leave for her interview. She had already texted Mindy to let her know that she was alright, and that she would call her later to let her know what was going on. She decided to wear one of the only two items she had brought from Jon's place. She put on the dangling earring she wore that night of the Fashion Show, hoping Mr. James would remember how good she had looked that night. She didn't want to get the job because she was trying to seduce Mr. James, but she figured any subliminal messaging couldn't hurt.

She arrived early at 10:30 am. She wanted to make sure she made a good impression by being prompt. She was wearing her light pink two piece suit and her skin tone heels. In her hand she carried a folder with a copy of her resume. She hoped that Jon wouldn't take offence that she had printed her resume on his printer the morning she had gone to pick up her stuff. Part of her felt guilty for using his printer, but she rationalized that if Jon had been using her simply for fun, it was a fair trade.

Alicia had never been to the corporate office of "From this Day Forward," so she didn't know what to compare this place to, but it was stunning. The white marble floor was polishes such at you could see your reflection. The walls were all a dark gray and the windows were covered with sheer white curtains. A chandelier hung down the center of the room and the secretary's desk was a light white wash color.

The bubbly lady behind the asked, "Hello, may I help you?"

Alicia tried to walk without slipping on this pristine glass surface. "Hello, I'm here for an 11 o'clock appointment with Mr. James."

Holly checked her schedule, "Alicia Garcia?"

Alicia smiled and nodded. "Yes, that's me."

Holly smiled back, "You're early. I'll let Mr. James know you are here. Please have a seat." She signaled towards the wall where the plush black chairs were located.

Alicia sat down and started to feel nervous. *What I am I doing? Is this the right thing to do? What if he offers me a job simply because he likes me not because he thinks I have talent?*

"Ms. Garcia, Mr. James will see you now." Holly stood at the office door and ushered her in.

Alicia walked in. This room was very different from the main waiting room. This was a man's office. The wall and floor where all made of cherry red wood. The desk matched the walls and there in the middle of this earthly room stood Mr. Max James.

"Hello Alicia, nice to see you again." He shook her hand. "Please have a seat."

"Thank you Mr. James." Alicia sat down and brushed her long brunette hair way from her face. "I brought my resume," she handed it to him.

Mr. James took it and perused it. "So you have worked in the wedding industry for over three years and before that as a sales representative for the cell phone industry." He looked up to glance at Alicia.

"Yes, I don't have any formal training in design, but I have learned plenty from being on the shop floor. For two years I had direct access to brides. Most of them knew what they were looking for. So I have learned what styles are more likely to be successful and which will not." Alicia tried to relax but it was hard with Mr. James eyes dissecting her.

"Yes, I noticed you had an eye for fashion the night we met. My question to you is why are you here? I mean I can't believe that Jon would let you leave his organization without offering you a better deal than Assistant Manager." Mr. James sat back trying to understand what was happening.

Alicia rigidly sat on the edge of her seat. She didn't want to discuss Jon, but she gave him a wry smile. "Let's just say that "From this Day Forward,' and I had a disagreement as to where I see my future going. Now, if I don't meet the qualifications for the position, I understand." Alicia stood up, "Thank you for your time, and consideration." She nodded and smiled.

Mr. James was astonished not only by her natural beauty but by her ability to handle herself in awkward situation. He knew he had asked a personal question, but he wanted to know why she would leave Jon. He had seen how she looked at him and how her face had lit up when Jon had kissed her. Mr. James leaned forward and picked up a pen from his desk, but he did not stand. Instead he sat there and looked up towards her giving her a sense of control. "Ms. Garcia, I did not say that you are not qualified for the position, I think you are more than qualified for the job. You are smart, eloquent, and have a way of making people feel comfortable around you. Plus, you intuitively posses an understanding of design, but you must understand I need to know why you have decided to leave 'From this Day Forward.' How can I trust you and your loyalty to this organization if you are not completely honest with me?"

Alicia sat back down. Once more she bushed her hair back exposing a dangling earring. *Sooner or later he's going to find out the truth. It's probably better if I tell him myself.* "Mr. James, I was demoted after I approved a $5,000 alteration on a wedding dress. The bride claimed she did not know that the request would be irreversible, but both I and the seamstress had expressed our concerns and unwillingness to do the changes. She insisted and we, I mean, I finally agreed. When she came in for a final fitting she accused me of destroying her dress."

"You mean to tell me that Jon was stupid enough to demote you?" his eyes almost popped out of his head and his mouth dropped open.

Alicia shook her head and averted her eyes. "No, it was his brother Steven."

Mr. James could see the pain in Alicia's face. "I'm sorry, things didn't work out the way you had expected, but I am pleased to have you here with us now. Before I offer you the job, you must understand that this position requires you travel a lot. There are many shows we must attend to stay up to date with the latest designs. Traveling is tedious, tiresome and downright boring, but it must be done. If you are willing to live half your life in hotels and airplanes, then I officially offer you the position of design consultant, if you are still interested in taking it." He stood up and put out his hand for a hand shake.

Alicia stood up and smiled. "Yes, Mr. James. I accept your job offer."

The sparkle in her eyes was alluring. Mr. James could stare into them all day. He willed himself to speak and break the hypnotic trance she had over him. "Now, I'll introduce you to the team you will be working with."

# Chapter 18: Money Isn't Everything

It had now been four months since she has started working for Mr. Max James. She was making three times the amount of money she had made as an Assistant Manager, and she had found that traveling wasn't as bad as it sounded, especially since she had never been out of Southern California in her entire life. She had met many people in the world of fashion, and loved working with Shelly and Daniela. She had moved into a small apartment in Altadena to be closer to her work. Her new place was only five minutes away from the office. Mindy and her stayed in contact via text and phone. She visited her mom and sister as often as she could. But she had not spoken to Jon since that day she was been demoted.

Jon had continued to call her at least once a week. He would say hello and hoped she was doing well, and then he would hang up.

As she sat at her small kitchen bar writing out the check for the car loan she thought of how much she missed Jon. Every month for the past four months, Alicia had written out a check to pay him back for the car loan. She knew that Jon received the checks, because he always emailed her to let her know that he had received them, but he never cashed them.

The pain this day was worse than any she had felt, she had just returned from the San Francisco Fashion Show with Mr. James and Shelly. Both Janet and Katrina had been in the show. After the show, they had spotted Alicia in the crowed and had smirked at her. They whispered to their friends, and everyone turned to stare. Alicia was furious, but knew that there was nothing she could do.

Mr. James had noticed how upset she had become when Janet and Katrina were talking behind her back. He had tried to cheer her up. She would never forget his kind words. "Their beauty is superficial. Your beauty radiates from within, and that's why they're jealous. They fear your strength and beauty."

Alicia new a come-on when she her it but she never felt any attraction towards Mr. James maybe because her heart would always belong to Jon. She did however think of him as a very kind man and a good friend.

She drove to the post office to drop off the check, before going in to work. The only thing that stopped her from drowning in tears was work. Every day she was away from Jon a piece of her soul died. She had become very good at numbing her feelings by throwing herself into work.

Mr. James watched Alicia as she walked through the main waiting room. He had noticed that Alicia had lost her vivacious luster. She was sadder now than the day she had started working for him. Life had become about closing the deal, not about enjoying her job. He had also noticed that Alicia wore the same earrings daily, the ones she had worn the night they met. He knew that they must have been a gift from Jon.

"Alicia, what are you doing here today? This is your day off. We just flew in last night. Please go home and rest." Mr. James insisted. Hoping she would go home and do something other than work.

"I just have a few phone calls to return, and then I'll head home," Alicia tried to smile but it was only a one sided smile.

"Alicia, I insist that you take a break! You need to do something with your life that isn't work related. You're making yourself miserable." Mr. James stood in front of her preventing her to enter her office.

Alicia's tenaciousness kicked in. "I might be coming down with the flu, that's why I look drained. I'm sure I'll feel better in the morning Mr. James. I promise to go home after I make these three phone calls."

Mr. James stepped out of her way. As she passed his side he grabbed her arm gently, "Alicia, I'm worried about you. Please tell me how I can help."

Alicia leaned her head and looked into his deep blue eyes. She saw concern and something else, something she had seen in Jon's eyes before desire. "I'll be fine Mr. James, I just need to go home and rest."

Max James was furious with Jon. *Why hasn't he come for her? Why is he making her suffer? Maybe he needs to have a fire lit under his ass!*

Max noticed how miserable Alicia looked. Over the months of working side by side with Alicia, he had realized she was stubborn and unwilling to back down. He knew she would never call Jon and tell him how she felt, even if it killed her. Max would have to reach out, if she wasn't willing to.

Max sat at his computer, downloaded pictures from the last few shows where he was standing next to Alicia holding a wine glass, and smiling for the camera. She looked as beautiful as ever, but with a hint of sadness in those honey eyes. He wrote a message that said, "She's not the same without you." He hit send before he could change his mind.

Max had hoped that Alicia would tire of waiting for Jon, and notice how he felt about her, but she had never shown an interest in him. Many times he has tried to get her to call him by his first name Max, but Alicia refuse and continued to address him as Mr. James. They had become work friends, but Alicia would not open up about her personal life. He had never pushed.

Half an hour later, the phone rang. Max picked up the phone. "Hello?"

"Max, it's Jon. Is she okay?" Jon asked over the phone.

"No, Jon she's not okay!" There was anger in his voice. "She's too dam stubborn to admit it, but she misses you. She's becoming hollow, drowning herself with work. It's killing her!" *And me!*

******

"I'm taking the next flight out. I'll see you in the morning." Jon hung up the phone. He walked out of his office and into Steven's office.

"Steven, I'm leaving for Altadena, California. I don't know when I'll be back so you're just going to have to run things until I can get back." He stood by his brother's desk fuming.

"What's going on? Why the rush?" Steven stared at Jon perplexed.

Jon walked over his bothers computer and opened the email with the pictures of Alicia and Max. "That's why! She's been working for Max James this whole time. He's had her at his side for four months and now he yells at me for making her miserable!"

Steven stood up and put his hand on his brother's shoulder. "Jon, please calm down. What are you planning on doing?"

"First, I'm going to ask her to forgive me for being stupid. I never should have asked you to let her go from her position. Then, I'm going to tell her I love her." Jon walked out of the office.

# Chapter 19: Time to Face the Truth

Alicia walked into the office hoping Mr. James would not notice her arrival. She had left like she had promised the day before, but now there were more calls that needed to be made.

Mr. James seemed to always know when she arrived and had made it a habit of stopping by her office and dropping off a cup of coffee. She was surprised when he had not yet brought a cup of coffee for her this morning, but she didn't give it much thought, she had phone calls to make.

Alicia's office phone rang, "Good morning this is Alicia Garcia. How can I be of assistance?"

"Alicia, Mr. James would like to see you in his office." Holly replied.

"Oh, did he sound upset?" Alicia asked as she stood up.

"Just come to the office, okay." Holly insisted.

*I hope Mr. James isn't mad that I'm here early again.* "Hi Holly, can I go in?"

Holly nodded.

Alicia ran her hand though her hair and put on a fake smile. "Good morning Mr. James. You wanted to see me?" She stepped into his office and saw Mr. James sitting at his desk. Then she saw him, still has handsome and as attractive as she remembered.

Jon stood to his feet, "Hello, Alicia." He didn't move afraid to spook her away.

Max stood up. "Alicia, please come in and close the door behind you."

Alicia was motionless. She could not understand what was happening. *How did he find me? Why is he here?*

Max walked over to the door, "I'll close the door for you, then. Alicia you are not to leave this office until you have heard Jon out. I've been watching you work yourself to the ground in order to hide the pain, and I can't take it anymore. I'm going to stand right outside this door, in case you need me." Max glared at Jon and closed the door behind him.

Alicia had heard every word that Mr. James had said, but she still didn't understand why Jon was here. "Why are you here?" she asked.

Jon walked up to Alicia. He gently moved her hair away from her beautiful eyes. "Because I've missed you," he whispered. "Alicia, I'm sorry for being so stupid. I wanted to surprise you with a store. Your own Franchise store but I was in Canada and couldn't tell you in person before you took off. I've been looking for you for months Alicia to tell you that I love you."

Alicia's eyes filled with tears. Had she heard him correctly? *Did he just say he loved me?* A faint smile came over her as she whispered, "I love you too."

Alicia took Jon's face in her hands, still unsure that he was really there. *Am I dreaming?* "Are you really here?" She looked into his hazel eyes, searching for the truth.

"I'm sorry for running away again," she said as the tears rolled down her face uncontrollably. "I've missed you so much."

Jon wrapped his arms around her waist and pulled her in close. He hated watching her cry. It tore a hole in his heart. Without removing his eyes from hers he said, "I've been going crazy hoping you would contact me. I've been lost without you Alicia. Mindy and Ceci are both tired of hearing from me. I've been calling them weekly looking for you."

"Then, how did you know I was here?" Alicia traced his lips with her fingers unable to figure out how he could have known if Mindy and Ceci had not told him.

Jon wiped the tears from her face. "Max contacted me yesterday," Jon replied with a hint of jealously. "He said he was worried about you. So I came to see you, hoping you would agree to see me so I could tell you how much you mean to me."

Alicia could see that he meant what he said. She leaned in for a soft sweet kiss. Oh, how she had missed his scent. She took a deep breath to take him in. She'd missed how his lips tasted. So she sucked on his bottom lip hungrily. She'd missed how his warm body felt up against hers, and she pulled in closer so there was no space between them. The tears continued to roll down her face.

Jon unwillingly pulled away, "Please Alicia don't cry, please."

Alicia tried to control her tears. She took a deep breath and wiped her face.

"I think we should continue this conversation, at your place and not in Max's office." Jon stated.

In the heat of the moment Alicia had forgotten where they were. She looked around, "Yes, we should probably give Max his office back."

Jon opened that door. "Max, will you please come back in."

As Max walked back into his office, he looked at Alicia. He could tell that she had been crying, and that angered him, but he could also see that the glimmer and shine was back in her eyes. The smile on her face was genuine. "Is everything okay?" He asked Alicia.

Alicia ran up to Max and gave him a huge hug. Then she kissed him on the cheek. "Thank you Max, for everything."

Max was stunned. This was the first time Alicia had addressed him as Max, or had shown any affection towards him. Speechless, he simply smiled at Alicia and nodded.

"There are some items we still need to discuss, would it be alright if Alicia took the rest of the day off?" Jon asked.

Max smiled, "She can take the rest of the week off. Now, that you two are on speaking terms, I doubt she will continue working for our company."

Again Alicia hugged Max. She pulled back and said, "You know. I think Shelly is ready to take on my responsibilities. I have been training her so that she could someday take over. I hope you won't be terribly upset with me, just leaving like this."

Max shook his head as he took Alicia's hand, and with a soft smile he said, "This is the happiest I have seen you in four months. I know you love your job, but there has to be more to life than work. I think you've always known that, but are too bullheaded to admit it. I will miss working with you, but I understand."

Max gave Jon a warning stare. Then he turned back at Alicia, "Know that I will always be here if you need a friend."

# Chapter 20: A Proposal

Jon followed Alicia back to her new apartment. This place was smaller than the apartment she had shared with Mindy. Alicia offered, "Would you like something to drink?" as she put her purse down on the small bar that divided the living room from the kitchenette.

"All I have is water and tea. I'm not here much, so I don't keep the fridge stocked." She pulled out two bottles of cool water and walked back into the living room where Jon stood.

"Thank you." Jon took the water bottle from her hand. "Alicia, can we sit and talk?"

Alicia sat next to Jon on her small love seat. She placed her bottle on the coffee table and took Jon's hand. "Jon, I'm sorry if I hurt you, but when I was demoted my survival instinct kicked in. I knew that if I spoke to you, I would not be able to leave you. I wasn't going to go back to being a clerk when I knew I had so much more to offer." She bowed her head in remorse. "And, I also thought you were simply using me as a distraction from your day to day life."

Jon felt those stabbing words penetrated his gut. His eyes filled with sadness. "Alicia, I'm sorry it took me so long to tell you that I love you. Every day since you left, I have wished I had told you the moment I realized it." He took her hand to his lips and kissed it.

Jon put the water bottle down on the coffee table, and kneeled down on one knee. "Alicia, I don't want to spend another moment without you. I love you more than life itself. Will you marry me?" He pulled out a beautiful solitaire engagement ring from his pocket."

Alicia looked at him completely overwhelmed. She was speechless. She nodded and finally found her voice, "Yes Jon, I'll marry you."

Jon took the ring and placed it on her finger. He stood up and pulled her towards him. He kissed her a kiss that left no doubt how he felt about her. They stood there kissing each other for a long time trying make up for lost time.

Jon ran his hand down her back igniting Alicia on fire. There wasn't a part of her body that didn't want Jon to take her right there. She moaned a long soft moan messaging her want.

Jon knew that signal, he had missed her subtle signs. He picked her up in his arms and asked, "Which door is your bedroom."

Alicia smiled, "The one on the right."

Jon carried her towards the door. She opened it. Jon let her down at the edge of the bed. In a gruff voice he blurted, "Alicia I want you. If you want me to stop, let me know now." He kissed her neck softly moving down towards her breast.

"Please, Jon don't stop," she responded as she leaned back and took a deep breath.

Jon quickly removed her blouse. He snapped her bra and exposed her already erect nipples. He groaned as he took her nipple into his mouth.

Alicia's inner thighs began to tingle. For the last four months Alicia had dreamt of having Jon inside her, and those dreams had felt so real, but this feeling was more intense. The way Jon's warm hands puller her in closer and the way his tongue teased her nipples, sent shock waves throughout her body. Alicia could feel herself dripping with want.

Alicia reached over to Jon's pants, unbuttoned his pants and dropped them along with his boxers. She quickly unzipped her skirt and slipped out of it. Jon helped remove her panties. Alicia laid back on the bed.

She looked at the man who stood there already at attention, and said, "Jon, I've missed you so much."

"Oh baby, I've missed you more than you can imagine." He climbed on the bed between her legs. He ran his hand between her thighs. "Mmm," he moaned feeling how wet she was. "Should we play first or skip the foreplay?"

Alicia's body yearned to be filled. She breathing was heavy and her heart was racing. She sat up and kissed him, "I want you in me now."

Jon grinned from ear to ear. "Then, we can play later." He slowing pushed his way in.

Alicia began to moan. With every thrust, her moaning became more erratic. Suddenly her uterus began to convulse. She wrapped her legs around Jon, and let out a load moan. Just then, Jon erupted inside her, and collapsed on top of her.

They lay there in each other's arms for some time. Jon finally lifted himself off her and asked, "Are you okay?"

Alicia smiled and nodded, "I'm better than okay."

Jon rolled to Alicia's side and kissed her on the cheek and placed his hand on her stomach. Then he asked, "Now that you're my fiancée are you going to stop sending me a check every month for your car?"

Alicia exploded into laughter. She had not laughed in such a long time she had forgotten what laughing felt like. "I'm going to keep on writing you a check until I have finished paying you for my car, and you can keep doing whatever it is you do with my checks." She ran her fingers through his hair.

Jon nibbled on her ear. "I place them in the top drawer of my office desk. That was the only connection I had to you, so I'd pull them out and look that them when I missed you."

Alicia's heart pained as she thought about how much hurt she had caused him. All because she had believed that Jon didn't care for her. "Did you look at them often?" She asked guiltily.

"Sometimes I'd look at them three or four times a day, but when I was on the road I'd stare at your picture." Jon whispered into her ear?

"Which picture?" Alicia didn't remember taking a picture with Jon.

"This one," Jon reached down to pick up his pants. He pulled out his phone and showed her the picture of him kissing her that night on the terrace when Steven had asked for proof.

Alicia's heart melted. *I can't believe he still has this picture.* "Jon, I love you." This time when she leaned in for a kiss, it was a hot passionate kiss.

# Chapter 21: The Bride

Alicia looked at herself in the large floor to ceiling mirror. She couldn't believe this was truly happening. Reflecting back at her was a radiant bride. She stood there staring at that white bohemian wedding dress she had fallen in love with last spring. The dress was French lace from top to bottom. Its sleek silhouette and deep v-neck showed off only a small part of her breast, just enough to tease. The eyelash lace details on the petal-hued lining gave the dress a subtle blush that draped to the floor, and the cap-sleeves seemed to kiss her shoulders.

Here she was one year later, getting ready to walk down the beach, to marry the most wonderful man in the world. *I'm getting married at Maluaka Beach. I can't believe this is really happening!*

"Alicia, are you ready?" Mindy asked as she came into the changing area. "All the guest have now seated." She handed Alicia the white and pink frangipani blossoms bouquet.

Alicia turned to face her Maid of Honor. She smiled at Mindy, "I think so. I have my bouquet. I have

something new," she patted her dress. "My something borrowed." She touched her veil. Cecilia had let her barrow her wedding veil for good luck. "My something blue," she patted her thigh where the blue garter belt sat.

Mindy hugged Alicia, "You look beautiful. Jon is going to die at the sight of you. I hope he can keep his hands off you long enough to make it through the ceremony."

Alicia shook her head and laughed. "You always know just what to say to make me feel better."

There was a knock at the door. "May we come in?" Cecila and their mother popped their heads into the room.

"Claro que si!" Alicia responded. Alicia hugged Ceci and her mom.

"Que bonita te vez hija," her mother said.

"You look so beautiful," she repeated as she spun her daughter around.

"Thank you mami, now let's go before the groom changes his mind," Alicia smirked.

Ceci laughed, "I doubt that will happen. Jon has been standing by the alter for almost two hours. He said he didn't want to be late for his own wedding. I think the sound of the crashing waves helps him relax, but he's not willing to admit it."

"Oh, I hope I didn't take too long to get ready." Alicia replied in a worried tone.

Mindy smiled and said, "You have never been late to anything. So I doubt you'll be late to your own wedding. Now let's go."

\*\*\*\*\*\*

As soon as the bride arrived everyone stood. The rose petal aisle directed Alicia straight down the beach to where Jon stood next to the minister and his brother Steven. In the front row stood Jon's mother and Father smiling.

First, the twins walked down the aisle carrying the rings. Then Cecilia as the Bride maid and Mindy and the Maid of Honor walked down the beach to the first row. They stood next to Sara. Finally, Alicia stood there with her mother by her side. The ukulele began to play as Alicia and her mom walked down the aisle. Alicia could not believe that Jon had paid for her entire family to join them in Maui. She felt like the luckiest women alive, and the smile on her have showed how blessed she felt.

When they arrived at the front her mom handed Jon Alicia's hand. Alicia looked into Jon's eye's and saw pure love.

"You look amazing," Jon whispered as he brought her hand up to his lips and kissed it.

Alicia felt herself blushing, but didn't say a word. She was afraid that if she opened her mouth the tears would start to follow.

The minister finally said, "Are you ready?"

Jon and Alicia turned to the minister and shook their heads.

"Dears friends and family today we have all come together to bear witness that true love is so pure and powerful that it can endure the challenges of life and withstand the test of time. Do you Jon take this women Alicia as your wife to honor and cherish for the rest of your life?"

Jon smiled, squeezed Alicia's hands and said, "I do."

The minister continued, "Do you Alicia take this man as your husband, to love, honor, and cherish for the rest of your life?"

Alicia's tears began to trickle down the side of her face and she smiled and said, "I do."

Jon took his handkerchief from his top pocket and wiped the tears way. "Are you okay?"

Alicia nodded, "Just tears of joy."

The minister continued. "The rings please. Jon, please repeat, 'With this ring I give you my heart... I have no greater gift to give... I promise I shall do my best to protect our love... I feel so honored to call you wife... and so blessed to call you mine.'"

Jon repeated and placed the ring upon Alicia's shaking hand.

Then minister turned to Alicia. "Alicia, please repeat, 'With this ring I give you my heart... I have no greater gift to give... I promise I shall do my best to protect our love… I feel so honored to call you husband… and so blessed to call you mine.'"

Alicia tried to hold back the tears and to repeat the words without a shaky voice, but she found it hard to speak up. She whispered the words as she tried controlling the joy she felt. Finally, she slipped her ring onto Jon's finger.

"By the power vested in me by God and the State of Hawaii, I now pronounce you husband and wife. You may now kiss the bride," the minister announced.

Jon didn't waist a moment. He scooped Alicia in his arms and kissed her will all the love in his heart.

Alicia's tears ran freely. "I love you Jon."

"I love you more," Jon replied with the smile.

The sun had begun to set. The clear blue water now glistened with hues of red and orange. The guest all walked up to the married couple for hugs and best wishes. Everyone walked back up to the hotel to continue the celebration on the outdoor reception area. The private luau would begin shortly.

# Chapter 22: A New Life

Alicia sat in her new corporate office staring at all the pictures on her favorite wall, pictures of the perfect beach wedding. A warm feeling filled her body as she sat there and stared at the center portrait, the one of her and Jon staring into each other's eyes with the backdrop of the Maui sunset. She wore Sue Kim's bohemian wedding dress, the dress she had fallen in love the first time she had attended the Bridal Fashion Show with Jon. Next to that picture was a picture of her and her wedding party, Mindy as the Maid of Honor, Ceci and as her Brides Maid and the twins as the ring bearers.

Next to that picture was a picture of her and Jon with the in-laws, her Mom to her left and Jon's parents to his right. Alicia thought of how accepting Jon's parents had been of her, knowing that she had nothing to offer their son but her heart. Jon's mother had told her, "Jon has all the money he can possibly need. Now he needs a wife that will make him happy, and I haven't seen Jon this happy since he discovered candy at age three."

Then there were pictures of the guests, but the most special guest picture of all was the picture of Max and Mindy sharing some champagne. Alicia could tell that they had hit it off. Secretly she hoped Mindy and Max would become a couple, but she had promised Jon not to meddle.

Jon walked into her office and said, "Hey babe Stevie wants to know if we're going to make the barbeque dinner tomorrow."

Alicia still couldn't believe she was married to the most amazing man in the world. "Let me check your schedule. Yes, I think we are clear for tomorrow evening. We don't need to be at the photo shoot for three more days."

"Okay, I'll let him know. Are we taking a side dish?" Jon asked as he bent down to kiss his new bride.

"Mmm, yes I'm planning on taking tostadas, with homemade beans." Alicia smiled as Jon started to laugh.

# About the Author

This is Alexandra Medini's first Romance Novella. She lives with her husband and kids in California. She enjoys reading as a past time, and has decided to writing a try. She hopes you enjoy this story.

# Notes

www.ingramcontent.com/pod-product-compliance
Lightning Source LLC
Chambersburg PA
CBHW020137180626
46810CB00004B/1609